The Curve of Chance

Vijay Raghav

ISBN 978-93-52010-02-8
Copyright © Vijay Raghav, 2017

First published in India 2017 by Inkstate Books
An imprint of Leadstart Publishing Pvt Ltd

Sales Office:
Unit No.25-26, Building No.A/1,
Near Wadala RTO,
Wadala (East), Mumbai – 400037 India
Phone: +91 96 99933000
Email: info@leadstartcorp.com
www.leadstartcorp.com

Disclaimer: The Views expressed in this book are those of the Author and do not pertain to be held by the Publisher.

Editor: Jayashree Aradhyam
Cover: Tina Patankar
Layouts: Logiciels Info Solutions Pvt. Ltd.

Printed at Dhote Offset

Dedicated to T.S. Ananda Rao

Also by Vijay Raghav

The Peak of all Thoughts

Fall

Contents

About the Author

Born in Chennai in 1983, Vijay Raghav studied engineering at Madras University and completed his Post Graduate studies in Business Management from Bharathidasan Institute of Management. A Technology professional in the day and a writer at heart, Vijay's literary career began as a poet in 2012 after he published his first book – The Peak of all Thoughts – a bouquet of poetic essays discussing various aspects of life written in prose–poetry style. He launched his debut novel *Fall* – a riveting story of love, envy, deceit and mystery – in 2013. He reads everything he can lay his hands on from Milan Kundera, Jiddu Krishnamurthy, Friedrich Nietzsche to Keigo Higashino, Stephen Hawking and Stephen King.

Acknowledgments

I am grateful to my editor, Jayashree Aradhyam, and my publisher, Lead Start Publishing House, for showing interest in my work.

I am indebted to Kanishka Gupta (Writers' side) for being an honest critique. Suggestions from his team improved my narrative and writing skills.

I am thankful to Nikhita Prabhudesai for her work on the book cover design.

It is likely that unlikely things should happen.

Aristotle

Prologue
The Confluence

Present Day

It was supposed to be a bit dark outside the airport, but the tall, new air traffic control tower stood like a blazing torch illuminating the scene. Numerous head- and tail-lights injected liveliness into the nightlife of the city. A network of street lights spread across the length and breadth of Mumbai brightened it, adding to the oft-repeated phrase: Mumbai never sleeps.

There was a sense of excitement in the air as the world was bidding farewell to the old year and gearing up to welcome the new. The year 2016 was just a few hours away and around half of Mumbai's population was welcoming it in a drunken haze by dancing and singing under electrifying disco lights. Migrants desperate to get to their hometowns were clogging the departure points: the airport, railway stations, bus stops and taxi stands. Outside the airport, dazzling fireworks decorated the dark sky with stunning colours. And inside the airport, the overall mood was upbeat.

Chhatrapati Shivaji International Airport was crowded and one could hear the constant chatter of people, the ringing of cell phones and the boarding announcements alerting passengers of the departure of their flights. High-quality duty-free merchandise in charming boutiques lured foreigners by offering great discounts. Many travellers were killing their free time by catching up with friends on Twitter or Facebook on their laptop computers using free Wi-Fi hotspots. Mobile phones were beeping and vibrating with New Year messages. Television screens were displaying the Breaking News stories of the day. One screen showed a new species of frog with a tail and the text scrolling across read: *Researchers in Congo discover new species of frog with tail measuring 7 cm. It is dark blue in colour and it has no tongue or teeth. It does not croak like normal frogs and remains silent. Nature astonishes us with endless surprises! It definitely seems to be an outlier!* Another screen showed news of the world's first successful full head transplant.

Abhishek Patil straightened his tie in the colours of the Indian flag and tied his shoestrings. He was well groomed; his shirt and trousers were clean and pressed to perfection. His attire was in accordance with the grooming policies of Air India for pilots and his face was etched with a pilot's wisdom. He walked through the security check-in with a smile on his face and adjusted his overcoat before speaking briefly to one of the air hostesses accompanying him. 'I am going to complete 20,000 flying hours soon,' he remarked. His voice brimmed with arrogance and pride.

Ten minutes later, a high-pitched voice emerged from the flight announcement system. *This is the pre-boarding announcement for flight AI 605 to New York. We are now inviting those passengers with small children, and any passengers requiring special assistance, to begin boarding at this time. Please have your boarding pass and identification ready. Regular boarding will begin in approximately twenty minutes' time. Thank you.*

Boeing 777-300, the metallic marvel, was standing at the gate. Patil spoke to the flight attendant about the weather conditions and ride reports. 'Everything is okay sir, we are good to go,' she said. 'Tell Rakesh to do the walk-around,' said Patil and went to grab a cup of coffee from the terminal before setting up his side of the cockpit.

Rakesh Mehra was the first officer on flight AI 605 and had been Patil's second-in-command for almost two years. He was the flying pilot, though Captain Patil was responsible for the aircraft, its passengers, and the crew. Being a long-haul flight, Jatin Doshi had been added to the crew as a relief pilot to assist Rakesh during his rest periods.

As instructed by the captain, Rakesh took a stroll and inspected the overall condition of the aircraft, checking the tire pressure, the status of the oxygen bottles in the cockpit, the wear on the brakes, the engine fan blades for any nicks, and finally eyed the entire airplane for fuel, oil or hydraulic leaks.

Suddenly, a hasty voice emerged from the flight announcement system. *This is the final boarding call for passengers Sudhir Shivaram, Murali Rao, Vandana Rao, Vinod Johri and Ram Johal on flight AI 605 to New York. Please proceed to Gate no. 3 immediately. The final checks are being completed and the captain will order for the doors of the aircraft to close in approximately ten minutes' time. I repeat. This is the final boarding call for Sudhir Shivaram, Murali Rao, Vandana Rao, Vinod Johri and Ram Johal booked on flight AI 605 to New York. Thank you.*

After hearing the announcement, Murali rose slowly to his feet and stooped slightly as he walked towards Gate no. 3. His wife ushered him towards the gate. Sudhir, who looked both ecstatic and tense, got up with a start and walked towards the gate with an ambitious heart.

Adjusting his wire-rimmed glasses that rested comfortably on his broad nose, Vinod walked towards the gate in a hurried manner; a feeling of freedom rejuvenated him. The rushed tone of voice alerting the passengers to board the flight didn't seem to bother Ram as he strolled casually, but seeing others running past him towards the gate made him nervous.

Meanwhile, in the cockpit, Patil and Rakesh tested their oxygen masks and inspected all the electrical circuit breakers to make sure they were in place. Engine fire detection systems were tested resulting in a bell sound that one might usually hear while boarding the airplane. Rakesh checked everything meticulously: Auxiliary fuel pump – Off, Flight controls – Free and correct, Instruments and Radios – checked and set, Landing gear position lights – Checked, Altimeter – Set, Directional gyro – Set, Fuel gauges – Checked, Trim – Set, Propeller – Exercise, Magnetos – Checked, Engine idle – Checked, Flaps – As required, Seat belts/shoulder harnesses – Fastened, Parking brake – Off, Doors and windows – Locked.

'Sir, we are good to go,' he said to Captain Patil and recited a lengthy, boring pre-flight announcement like a school kid who'd been told to recite multiplication tables. *Ladies and gentleman, welcome onboard Flight AI 605 with non- stop service from Mumbai to New York. We are currently fourth in line for take-off and are expected to be in the air in approximately ten minutes' time. We ask that you fasten your seatbelts at this time and secure all baggage underneath your seat or in the overhead compartments. We also ask that your seats and table trays remain in the upright position for take-off. Please turn off all personal electronic devices, including laptops and cell phones or set your electronic devices to airplane mode until an announcement is made upon arrival. Smoking is not allowed on board, including in the lavatories.*

Also, use of electronic cigarettes is not allowed. Tampering with, disabling or destroying the smoke detectors in the lavatories is prohibited by law.

One of the air hostesses signalled to the other flight attendants to stand in their respective places, equidistant from each other and when they were ready to enact her words into actions, she addressed the passengers on safety measures, her voice soft and sweet like a fine wine.

Ladies and gentlemen, on behalf of the crew I ask that you please direct your attention to the monitors above as we review the emergency procedures. There are six emergency exits on this aircraft. Take a minute to locate the exit closest to you. Note that the nearest exit may be behind you. Count the number of rows to this exit.

Vinod adjusted his glasses and peered through them to locate his nearest exit.

In the event of an emergency, please assume the bracing position. Lean forward with your hands on top of your head and your elbows against your thighs. Ensure your feet are flat on the floor. Should the cabin experience sudden pressure loss, stay calm and listen for instructions from the cabin crew. Oxygen masks will drop down from above your seat. Place the mask over your mouth and nose, like this.

Sudhir, being a mountaineer, chuckled at the sight of the air hostess keeping the oxygen mask over her mouth and nose, for he had survived at high altitudes all his life and was not scared of heights. He was an expert in dealing with danger and his source of courage came from the moments he had spent with venomous snakes.

Pull the strap to tighten it. If you are travelling with children, make sure that your own mask is on first before helping your children. In the unlikely event of an emergency landing and evacuation, leave your carry-on items behind. A life vest is located in a pouch under your seat or between the armrests. When instructed to do so, open the plastic pouch and remove the vest. Slip it over your head. Pass the straps around your waist and adjust at the front. To inflate the vest, pull firmly on the red cord, only when leaving the aircraft. If you need to refill the vest, blow into the mouthpieces.

Ram Johal looked at the hip of one of the air hostesses standing near him. A bunch of young girls sitting behind Ram Johal were discussing plane crashes. 'Airplanes are safe and they are not risky,' remarked one of the girls and her claim was immediately refuted by the others. 'Of course flying is risky. Every time you sit on the plane, you expose yourself to chaos. Some planes crash during take-off and some crash in mid-air. There are as many as 10,00000 parts and the engineers put them all together to form an aeroplane. Even if one part fails, we are doomed! We will be killed in one place!'

An old woman who overheard their conversation told them to pay heed to the safety instructions and advised them to refrain from negative thoughts. 'Everything that happens in this world, even this air travel, is a part of God's plan. He can peep into the future and alter the course of events. So be optimistic and trust in his ways. Don't be pessimistic! Nowadays, you don't have to speak of the devil for it to appear, even if you think about it, it appears!'

*****

Story 1

Chapter 1: Thought Camera

Some months earlier

The weather was gloomy and the sky was a dull grey. Dark rain clouds carried watery white crystals in their wombs. A sticky breeze from the Arabian Sea swirled the dust into mini tornados, making it difficult for pedestrians to see and walk. A shabbily attired postman entered a deserted street near Bandstand Promenade, Bandra. Big bungalows stood on either side of the street, sticking to the sidewalks owned by poor people living in poverty. Two street dogs, one with an amputated leg and the other with a torn ear, followed the postman as he entered the main gate of one of them.

A watchman with a handlebar moustache stopped the postman and gave him an inquisitive look. He tilted his head sideways, leaning to his right and saw two dogs standing with saliva dripping from their tongues. Suddenly, the postman heard a sharp cry from directly behind him. The dogs yelped in pain after being beaten by the moustached watchman.

'Letter for Vinod Johri,' the postman said.

It was a big brown envelope with a government seal on it. *Department of Science & Technology* was printed in red ink on both sides with a *Confidential* tag. By all means, it was an important letter.

The watchman took the letter from the postman, crept up the stairs and knocked on the laboratory door. Joshi answered.

'How many times have I told you not to come here … You don't understand …'

'Letter for Saab,' the watchman said, interrupting his stream of words.

Pocketing the letter, Joshi walked towards the sliding door that opened to a passage leading to Vinod's living room. A postgraduate in Physics, Joshi had begun his career as a laboratory assistant to Vinod Johri in 2008. In college, he'd had a brilliant run, winning many medals and accolades. He'd graduated with flying colours and bagged the Outstanding Student award. Gold medals had earned him the respect and praise of colleagues and professors, but not money. While he roamed the streets of Mumbai without a job, the respect from others slowly turned into sympathy. Nobody saw the brilliant student in him and after three straight years of unemployment, he realised that education was not all that you needed to make money. Sometimes he'd lie awake at night, dreaming about getting a good job and living a luxurious life.

It was Vinod who'd given him new life by hiring him as a lab assistant. After mentoring him for two years, he had got him a job at the Tata Institute of Fundamental Research. He also trained him in interdisciplinary fields, like Biophysics and Neurophysics. His monetary status improved but he failed to learn the art of regulating his finances after marriage. Like his boss, he found himself in pressing need of cash all the time.

'There's a letter for you, sir – it's from the Department of Science & Technology,' Joshi said.

Vinod was sitting by the window, sipping ginger tea. His face looked as gloomy as the weather outside. He looked at Joshi through his wire-rimmed glasses and gestured that he read the letter.

Joshi tore open the envelope. He re-read the words, not believing his eyes. It was a carrier of bad news.

Vinod felt dispirited as his dreams had been shattered for the second time in a row. The first time had been exactly a year earlier, when the Department of Science & Technology rejected his research project along with his proposal requesting them to provide support and grants-in-aid to his ambitious experimental research in high-temperature superconductivity and nanophotonics. The Director of TIFR, having heard of his efforts in the field of nanophotonics, consoled him and his team of twenty scientists (including Joshi) and told them not to lose hope.

Moved by their words of encouragement, Vinod began his research in quantum physics. He worked relentlessly, doing experiments on tiny particles to create quantum computers that would harness the power of atoms and molecules to perform mathematical calculations significantly faster than any silicon-chip-based device. Unfortunately all his efforts were in vain: the Department of Science and Technology refused to financially support his research project and gave him their reasons in a courteous denial letter.

'Our grant application had all the traits to qualify for funding, and yet they rejected it. Hope is an empty word,' said Vinod, and tore the letter to pieces. He couldn't believe what was happening.

'Sir, we should not lose hope. You should speak to Mr Rao to give some momentum to this project,' Joshi said.

Vinod smiled, but it was not a happy smile. It was a sad smile. A smile so sad that even tears couldn't match its depth.

***

Dejected by the news, Joshi walked home. He stood before the door of his small house and knocked. When it opened, he entered and greeted his wife in a despondent manner, and sat between his children who were playing with cheap toys. The sound of a distant train made his children giggle with joy. His wife had the meal ready and they sat at a flimsy plastic table, eating their food.

'We'll have to buy a sturdy wood table,' she said.

'We will buy it next month,' he said quietly, nodding his head like a mechanical robot.

'Oh come on!' his wife said. 'This next month is never going to come … I have lost patience!'

'There's no money left at the end of the month because you haven't checked your spending habits,' Joshi snapped. Their argument about money turned into a full-blown fight and it took a while for their emotions to settle down. After eating dinner they stood on the balcony and talked of the day's events.

'You say you work for a prestigious research institute but the fact is that the *vada pav* man near Victoria Terminus earns more than you do,' his wife said.

'What do you want me to do? Sell *vada pav*?'

'Don't shout at me! Shout at your boss for not giving you a pay raise!' she yelled back. 'You've been working for him for seven years without any promotion or raise.'

'Get out of my sight before I slap you!' Joshi said.

She left, but what she had said haunted him. Her words echoed in his ears like a sermon. His mind rubbished her words but his heart accepted them as wise, true. Vinod wasn't good at selling himself and he had never had a knack for making money. His subordinates desperately needed some extra cash. Joshi had even asked Vinod to seek out a commercialisation approach to increase his chance of making some money but he had never understood his revenue potential. On the other hand, his father had known a lot about money and had amassed a fortune at a very young age. Upon his father's death, he had inherited a large portion of his wealth but failed to keep it intact. He had lost a huge chunk of money in his dramatic attempt to change the future of quantum physics and if Joshi hadn't stopped him, he would have pledged his Bandra bungalow to repay his scientific debts.

Joshi's problem was that he worked for a man of little luck. At times, to overcome his inharmonious, negative state of mind, he would visit his best friend Ahmed. Now, after a fight with his wife, he thought it was necessary for him to go out and meet him.

***

Ahmed placed a bottle of chilled sparkling wine on the table in front of Joshi. He found a soft cotton cloth and used it to dry the bottle. With his left hand, he grasped the neck of the bottle with four fingers and placed his right thumb over the top of the basket. Then he twisted the retaining wire in a counter-clockwise direction and tilted the bottle at a 45 degree angle. After a few seconds of twisting and turning, Joshi heard a gentle sigh as Ahmed allowed the cork to slowly ease out of the bottle's neck.

Joshi was impressed. 'Where did you learn all this?' he asked.

Ahmed poured a small amount of sparkling wine into a champagne flute and waited for the initial bubbles to subside before pouring more.

'Please,' Ahmed said, gesturing to the glass.

Joshi grinned and took one.

'Brachetto – Italian wine, costly stuff,' said Ahmed.

Joshi took a sip of his wine and smacked his lips.

'Five thousand rupees,' Ahmed said.

'You paid five thousand bucks for a bottle of wine!' Joshi gasped.

'No! My boss gifted me this wine … I do a lot of things for him,' Ahmed said.

'What's his name?'

'Hanif Abbasi,' said Ahmed, pouring a generous measure of sparkling wine into his glass.

'And what made him gift you such costly stuff?'

'I do a lot of risky jobs for him. All illegal stuff and, by the way, keep our conversation in confidence.'

'Don't worry Ahmed, what we speak about will not go beyond these four walls,' Joshi said. 'Your boss seems to be some kind of big shot.'

'Yes, he's a successful businessman and a cunning politician. No, sorry, I got it wrong, he's a cunning businessman and a successful politician,' said Ahmed and took a sip.

Joshi had never tasted such costly wine. He finished his first round in a jiffy and held up his glass for more. Ahmed opened the fridge, brought out another bottle of chilled sparkling wine, and did the opening-of-the-bottle act again.

'You have a minibar in your fridge, Bhai! You are a rich man now!' said Joshi, smiling and showing his yellow teeth. He noticed a thick gold chain shining amidst Ahmed's bushy chest hair.

Ahmed was a tall man, with a caste mark on his forehead. His beard was grey and bushy. He worked as a personal assistant to Hanif Abbasi. Joshi was interested to know more about Ahmed's boss, not because Ahmed served him costly sparkling wine but because of the sudden wealth he had stumbled upon after he started working for him.

Abbasi, a liquor baron from Maharashtra, had started his business at the age of ten, when his father managed to get a license to run a liquor store. After his father's sudden demise, Abbasi took over the business and within two years, he owned four country-made liquor shops in Vashi. He made significant profits by acquiring a license to sell alcohol wholesale throughout the state. Within nine years, he had expanded his business to 30 billion rupees in two states of western India, Maharashtra and Goa. In Mumbai alone, Abbasi owned 20 beer stores, 98 country liquor stores and 120 foreign liquor stores. He had also served as the Deputy Mayor of Thane Municipal Corporation for two years. Using his political clout, he exercised control over the liquor business in Maharashtra and his interests now spanned real estate, film production and pharmaceuticals.

'Your chief is really a big shot,' said Joshi.

'How is life treating you?' Ahmed asked, looking at Joshi with drooping eyes.

His question evinced no reaction from Joshi. He wanted to say 'Life is good!' with a happy, plastic smile, but he couldn't lie to his friend. The chilled wine that he had gulped a minute back acted upon him like a truth serum. He had no reason to hide things from Ahmed who had stood by him in tough times, who flunked in all subjects that he appeared for, who had roamed the streets of Mumbai without a job, who had been nothing but a pauper – and now, he sat in front of Joshi wearing a thick gold chain and a lot of money in his pocket.

Joshi told him everything. He told him things that weren't supposed to be told.

He told him about his poor financial status.

He told him about his boss.

He told him about the letter.

He told him about his pressing need for money.

And finally, he told him about the Thought Projector.

On hearing his words, Ahmed sobered up at once, and sat astonished. He couldn't speak for a while.

***

It was lunchtime. Mr Rao, Director of TIFR, was sitting next to his favourite window in his cabin. A stainless-steel tiffin-carrier with number 23 painted in green on its top was kept on his snack table. The lowest of the three tiers was packed with hot *jeera* rice, the middle contained spicy *dal tadka* and the top was filled with seedless black grapes. He had just begun to eat when he heard someone knocking on the door.

'Come in,' Rao said.

It was Vinod Johri. He sat opposite Mr Rao and gave him a dull smile.

'Did you get to talk to the top officials? Any luck with the funding?' asked Vinod.

Mr Rao gave a long-drawn-out speech. 'Nowadays, the Indian government is not providing enough money for scientific research. We have subcritical funding when it comes to allocation of money for science. These politicians are taking away all the money! Our country's policy on science and technology is a big joke! They don't invest in anything. High-temperature superconductivity, nanophotonics, quantum computers – these things don't mean a thing to the common man. All he wants is food and shelter. If you want to really flex your brain muscles, you should go to America or Japan or China. The Chinese and Koreans are racing each other to beat the US when it comes to investing heavily in science and technology, and we have been left far behind. And, mark my words, starting next year, the Chinese will beat the US.'

'Is there a way out? Can something be done to kick-start our projects?' questioned Vinod.

Mr Rao plucked a grape from the cluster and popped it into his mouth. 'It's not going to work. I don't think DST will support us.'

'What can we do now?'

'We can try contacting private companies for help,' Mr Rao said.

'Private companies always expect immediate profits,' said Vinod. 'I don't think it's a good idea, but I'll try ... '

Mr Rao ate a spoon of *dal tadka* mixed with *jeera rice* and said, 'All the best, Vinod! I can connect you to some of my contacts who might be of help to you. You can try your luck in pitching your research proposal to them but the chances of receiving funding from them seem very vague. Sorry! I don't want to sound pessimistic but that's the truth!'

Vinod approached many private companies, both national and multinational, to see his treasured projects take wing. He forced them, requested them and on some occasions, he pleaded with them to fund his projects. But they were not ready to help him.

***

John Anderson, Chief Executive Officer of the American Psychological Association (APA), adjusted his microphone and spoke. His voice was high-pitched and carried into crowds beautifully.

The theory that depression is a genetic brain disorder is wrong! Some say it is caused by unhealthy gut bacteria and some say it is due to chemical imbalance in the brain. The most interesting yet disturbing fact about depression and other psychological disorders is that people living in wealthier nations are more likely to have experienced depression than those in underdeveloped and developing countries. More than 20 million people in the United States alone suffer from depression in a given year and as many as 15% of those who suffer take their lives. The World Health Organization estimates that depression will be the second highest medical cause of disability by the year 2030, second only to HIV/AIDS.

Vinod increased the volume of the TV and the living room echoed with John's voice. Discovery Channel was airing his speech as a special segment. Vinod adjusted his glasses and sat glued to the screen as John continued.

Depression or major depression is a prolonged state of low mood where one has lost his sense of well-being. Depression and negative thinking are linked in a vicious circle. If you are feeling sad, you are likely to have lots of negative thoughts. And if you have lots of negative thoughts then you are bound to feel sad. It's like the story of the chicken and the egg. The human mind is naught but a honeycomb of thoughts with each cell indicating a unique thought. And if those thoughts turn out to be negative and if you keep rehashing them, you'll end up in depression.

There's also a link between depression and mental disorders. What makes someone lose their mind? We don't have any definite answers. The causes of mental disorders are often vague and even the diagnosis is made using an unstructured open-ended approach.

Vinod sat slouched on a chair, but he got up with a start. His eyes for some reason gleamed with delight. And he reacted as if he had a solution to all mental problems.

Everyone is fighting depression with antidepressants, but they are inefficient and sometimes don't work. Most patients taking antidepressants don't respond positively and they end up suffering from one or more side effects, including sexual dysfunction, fatigue, nausea, sleep disorder and weight gain.

Recent research suggests that low levels of melatonin cause depression. Some doctors say that excess mercury in the body is the culprit. But I think it's all in our mind ... in our thoughts!

'It's all in our mind ... in our thoughts!' repeated Vinod. 'That's goddamn right!'

Though we have been fighting depression, anxiety and other psychological disorders, they keep coming back! There seems to be no way out! The mind is a complex thing to deal with ... and thought is a heavy word to digest. There has to be some research into non-pharmaceutical treatments for depression.

After half an hour, John concluded his speech with a touch of humour. *I wish I could get hold of some portable helmet, which when worn could project vivid images of all that we think onto a big screen!*

After hearing him speak about portable helmets, the audience laughed but Vinod didn't. He knew that such portable helmets could be made. Then the audience responded to John's in-depth knowledge about psychological disorders with a stormy applause.

Vinod turned off the TV and googled John Anderson. A long forgotten event haunted him and he thought of reviving the phoenix from the ashes. Flashes of memory flickered in front of his eyes. The sound of breaking glass filled his mind. He remembered his days of hard work and the result that it had yielded; it was his obsession, his scientific dream, the product of his passion. He wanted to relive those days.

A new motive tingled in him and forced him to revive his past accomplishments.

***

In Abbasi's bedroom, lavish furniture and plush pillows gave the feeling of being in a luxurious private sanctuary full of peace and tranquillity. A crystal chandelier illuminated the room in a dull blue. A fire ant walked across the window-sill, and sniffed a fine white powder heaped like a small mountain. It was cocaine. The ant moved away from the powder after tasting it and now, it was Abbasi's turn to snort it.

Abbasi took a crisp 1000-rupee note from his pocket and rolled it into a tube. To crush the white powder as fine as possible, he took two credit cards from his wallet and rubbed one onto the other with some cocaine between. He then pushed the 1000-rupee straw deep into his nose and inhaled the powder with a sniffing sound. Bliss!

After ten minutes of sniffing and snorting, he rinsed his nose with salt water and walked to and fro in search of his cell phone. After five minutes of intense search, he found his phone lying under his plush pillow. He saw ten missed calls from Ahmed.

Just then the cell phone vibrated and it was Ahmed, calling him for the eleventh time.

'What's the matter?' asked Abbasi.

'Boss, I wanted to tell you something very important. Can we talk now?' Ahmed asked. He couldn't seem to contain his excitement.

'Let's not discuss it over the phone,' said Abbasi. 'Come home.'

In his 25 years of doing business, he had never discussed important, confidential matters over the phone. He had read about the effectiveness of phone taps in bringing down drug kingpins and criminals. For Abbasi, getting into the cocaine business had been a natural and profitable choice. To him, coke and liquor were like blood brothers, akin to each other as they both induced hallucination and forced all the crazy maniacs consuming them to lose themselves.

Ten years of dealing drugs and liquor had taken a toll on his sleeping habits, leaving him restless and irritated throughout the day. He paced the floor nervously, with a cigar in his mouth, waiting for Ahmed to arrive.

When the doorbell trilled, Abbasi opened it to see Ahmed, who looked visibly happy.

'What's the matter?'

'I can't believe what I heard from my friend,' said Ahmed, and after hearing him out, Abbasi was convinced that he was blabbering. He couldn't believe his words.

'Were you high on drinks?' asked Abbasi.

***

The concept of the Thought Projector had first become popular when it appeared in a *Fantastic Four* comic, way back in 1964. On a serious note, the idea of projecting thoughts as images was first conceived by Nikola Tesla. In the year 1933, a popular newspaper carried the news of Tesla's theoretical invention, the thought camera, which could photograph thoughts. When he was asked to comment on it, he had said, *In a time not distant, it will be possible to flash any image formed in thought on a screen and render it visible at any place desired.*

In the late summer of 2013, a new invention was built, the Thought Projector. It was an improved version of Tesla's theoretical thought camera and it was the next big thing! Only two living people knew about it – Vinod, who invented it and Joshi, on whom it had been tested. The inquisitiveness to read others' thoughts fuelled Vinod's grey matter and motivated him to create an improved version of Tesla's vision. And the moment he saw Joshi's thoughts being transformed into an image in front of his eyes, he was convinced that this was his best invention.

When Joshi witnessed this spectacular invention, he was flabbergasted. It looked like a compact eyeglass which had a sensor (apparatus) fitted onto its side. The sensor was connected to a tiny projector built into the other side of the glass. Though it looked like a compact eyeglass, it was not held at the temples and was not resting over the ears. It looked like skydiving glasses that could be fastened to the back of one's head. A tiny button was located on the side of the glass, near the sensor, which when pressed activated the sensor and made it emit an invisible beam that read the images on the retina and decoded people's thoughts by scanning blobs of brain activity. To give birth to his thought reading apparatus Vinod worked tirelessly, all night, taking almost no breaks.

Vinod destroyed his thought reading apparatus soon after he created it. Joshi was shocked to see Vinod destroying his own creation. Initially, the challenge to bring thought reading from the realms of fantasy to fact and a profound interest in his own work had motivated him to create an out-of-this-world invention, but at a later stage, Vinod had dropped the plan of making it public and refused to release his invention for the fear of it falling into the wrong hands and being used for evil.

***

It was a moonless night. Crickets were chirping loudly. The stars twinkled and some of them flickered as if they were playing hide and seek with those who were looking at them. The street near Bandstand Promenade was empty. There was an eerie silence. The clock in Vinod's laboratory gonged nine times, waking Joshi from his polyphasic sleep.

Vinod was wearing a grey coat and was sitting on a tall wooden stool, probing tiny atoms and molecules under an electron microscope. A cup of hot lemon tea was kept at his side. Time and again, Joshi looked at the telephone. He was expecting an important call.

Just then, the telephone rang.

Joshi wanted him to answer the call and accept the offer. He was prophesying a suitcase full of money and expected things to happen according to his plan but his inner self told him that it wouldn't. Like all highly eccentric geniuses, Vinod had no sense for handling money.

After a few rings, Vinod answered the call and sighed resignedly.

'Can I speak to Mr Vinod Johri?' said an unfamiliar voice.

'Yes, Vinod here.'

'I am so sorry to bother you at this time of the night … '

'That's okay,' said Vinod.

'My name is Ahmed. My boss would like to have a chat with you.'

'Who is your boss? Please ask him to call me tomorrow morning. I'm busy right now,' said Vinod.

'I mean, he wants to meet you in person.'

'All right, tell him to meet me at my office tomorrow morning at 10:00,' said Vinod.

'My boss would like you to visit him tomorrow at his guest house in Alibaug.'

Some stranger calling him at 9 p.m. and telling him to travel to Alibaug the next day to meet another stranger bewildered him.

'Mister, you are wasting my time! I am Vinod Johri, a very senior scientist! I think you have the wrong number.'

Ahmed continued his speech in a persuasive tone. 'Sir, I'll arrange for the travel. We can take the ferry from the Gateway of India to Mandawa Jetty and from there, my boss has arranged for a chauffeur-driven air-conditioned car, which will take us to his guest house in 20 minutes.'

'Can you tell me who your boss is?' asked Vinod.

'His name is Hanif Abbasi. You must have heard it ... he is quite popular.'

Vinod was completely taken aback. He had seen Abbasi's photo in the newspapers and had heard him speaking on news channels, always saying something about doing good for society.

'Why does Hanif Abbasi want to meet me?' he asked.

'Mr Abbasi would like to discuss a possible deal with you.'

'What deal? I am not a businessman. I am a scientist.'

'Sir, my boss is very anxious to meet you.'

'Mister Ahmed, don't waste my time. I am already occupied with a lot of things,' said Vinod.

'My boss wants to help you out with resuming your stalled research. I think you should meet him.'

Vinod was shocked. 'What are you talking about?' he stuttered.

'Sir, I don't want to sound suspicious, but it will be great if you can make it to Alibaug tomorrow.'

'Let me think about it. I'll give you a call in the morning.'

'Thank you!'

Vinod slammed down the phone, looked at Joshi with raging eyes and spoke in an angry tone. 'Did you tell anyone about our stalled research?'

It took some time for Joshi to answer. He felt like a lamb cornered by a wolf. 'I've not uttered a word about our projects to anyone. Is there a problem?'

***

A black-and-yellow taxi honked down a narrow, crowded street near the Gateway of India. Every commuter on that crowded street seemed to have his own traffic rules. Joshi was sitting in the front seat near the taxi driver and Vinod was sitting behind, thinking about the late night caller and his offer. A rich liquor baron wanting to make a deal and willing to kick-start his stalled projects somehow didn't fit in the scheme of things.

Once again, Vinod looked at Joshi with suspicion and asked, 'Did you tell anyone about our stalled research projects?'

'No sir, not at all.'

For the first time in his seven years of working with Vinod, Joshi had lied. He had done it without a second thought.

After 45 minutes of travelling through narrow streets, bumpy roads and jostling crowds, the cab stopped near Apollo Bunder. The air smelled of omelette *pav* and the sea.

Ahmed was standing at the designated place. Street hawkers were selling peanuts, and he took a palmful of them from the stuffed paper cone and popped them, one by one, into his mouth. Just then, the cell phone in his front pocket vibrated. He attended the call and heard Vinod's voice.

'Meet me near Gateway of India,' Ahmed answered, munching the peanuts.

It was noon. The weather was breezy and the sun was hiding behind thick white clouds. Vinod and Joshi met Ahmed near the Gateway of India and Ahmed behaved as if he were seeing Joshi for the first time.

'Hi! I am Ahmed, Abbasi's personal assistant,' said Ahmed, shaking hands with them. He ushered them to the place where the ferry service was offered. At a quarter past twelve, the ferry started. Vinod and Joshi sat on the lower deck of the ferry and Ahmed remained standing.

'First time to Alibaug?' asked Ahmed.

'Yes,' said Vinod and realised that it had been a long time since he ventured out of his lab. He slept only for four hours a day and sometimes worked through the night, engrossed in his experiments, and his passion had turned him into a loner with few friends.

Throughout the journey, Vinod remained tight-lipped. He half-smiled when Ahmed spoke to him about the weather, but mostly he maintained a sombre, scientist-at-work expression. It took them an hour to reach Mandwa Jetty, and from there, they got into a chauffeur-driven car. Ahmed sat next to the driver and signalled to him to start while Vinod and Joshi took the back seat.

'Do you live here?' asked Vinod, leaning towards Ahmed.

'No. I am a *Mumbaikar* and my boss is also a *Mumbaikar*. He conducts all his business deals here,' replied Ahmed. 'And this is a nice place to get away from city.'

After a smooth ride, the car took a sharp turn, waking Joshi from his afternoon siesta as it entered a deserted street.

'Do you know anything about the deal your boss is talking about?' asked Vinod.

'No,' said Ahmed. 'But I think my boss wants to help you.'

'What help? What does he want from me? What's the deal all about?'

Though Joshi knew everything about the deal, he sat mutely next to Vinod.

Ahmed didn't reply. The car stopped near a big bungalow.

Knowing his boss inside-out, Joshi could guess what would transpire between Abbasi and Vinod. Nevertheless, he wanted things to happen his way. He wanted Vinod to accept the deal. He tried filling his mind with positive thoughts but the image of Vinod taking a small hammer from his kit and shattering his own path-breaking invention haunted him. Joshi had tried to stop him but when Vinod blurted out why he had done it, he understood that Vinod – a man of principles – would live and die for them rather than doing or accepting something for the sake of money.

The posh bungalow with its landscaped garden and swimming pool was far from the hustle and bustle of the big city. Vinod and Joshi followed Ahmed as he pushed the front door of the bungalow open and entered the living room.

Vinod immediately recognised Abbasi from various news videos which he had recently seen on the Internet. He was fair-skinned and tall. His clean-shaven face gave him the perfect business executive look. He had a well-built physique, with shoulders like boulders – strong and rounded. His neatly pressed grey trousers and white shirt shone along with his thick black hair - neatly oiled and combed straight back.

'I am Hanif Abbasi,' he said. 'Thank you for accepting my invitation.'

'I'm Vinod Johri and this is my assistant Manohar Joshi.'

Ahmed stood behind Abbasi like an obedient assistant.

'Ahmed will take you to the guest room. You can freshen up and after that we can have lunch,' said Abbasi.

'I am not sure whether I'll have lunch here and it depends on what the so-called deal is all about,' said Vinod.

'In that case, I'll get straight to the point. I request you to listen to my words carefully and pay attention to everything I say before you make up your mind. I know you are a scientist, and I want to help you with resuming two of your stalled research projects by funding them,' said Abbasi.

Vinod was taken aback for the second time. The question of who might have told Abbasi about the stalled projects haunted him. He dropped his fruitless attempts to conceal information about his stalled projects and gave in to Abbasi.

'Why would you do that?' asked Vinod. 'And what would you gain from doing that?'

Abbasi gave him a wry smile. 'I don't want to beat around the bush with you. I'll tell you what I want. But before that, I want you to know more about me and my business.

'Okay,' said Vinod. And Joshi, who was standing behind Vinod was sweating profusely.

'As you know, I have been in the liquor business for the past twenty five years. Trust me, it is not an easy one. People are difficult to deal with. You have to bribe the police to get licences and, to sell liquor in any state, you need to maintain good relationships with the government officials. My brief stint in politics helped me do that. I never went to school but today I'm the King of Liquor in Maharashtra. I've had my setbacks when I ventured into real estate, film production and the pharmaceutical business. You know, in the world of business people conceal their real identities. Behind the mask, you will find their true intentions. You have to find the right partner to do business. But finding this person, someone without a mask, is very difficult and next to impossible in today's competitive world. I am not being sentimental here. I am no good man. In business, no one can be a good man. When people sign a business deal, they smile, they seem to be very genuine, but their intention is to pull you down. My own brother did that to me when he tried to kill me. He wanted my money. To cut a long story short, I want your Thought Glasses. I want to read others' thoughts. I want to rip them naked and see their real face. I want to be number one you see ... the number one businessman in Maharashtra ... number one in India.'

'I don't understand what you're saying ... what thought glasses are you talking about?' asked Vinod.

Abbasi gave a mischievous smile. 'I wish I had one in my hand right now to show your acting prowess to the world,' he said.

Vinod sat silent, dazed by everything that was happening around him. After collecting himself, he turned back and stared at Joshi, who was wiping beads of sweat from his forehead. Vinod instantly understood that Joshi had breached his trust.

'I won't talk about this to anyone. Everything that we spoke about will remain within these four walls and restricted to the four of us. You have to trust me,' said Abbasi in an assured tone of voice.

'I don't have the glasses with me. I destroyed my invention,' said Vinod.

'I know that. I want you to create them again for me. They will be a powerful tool in my hand and help me know what people really think and who they really are,' said Abbasi and Vinod noticed the change in his tone. It was no longer soft and pleasing but commanding.

'I don't want to take your deal and I am not going to recreate my invention!' said Vinod.

'If you accept the deal, then apart from funding your research projects, I'll give you 20 crores,' said Abbasi.

This made Joshi's eyes gleam. A simple "yes" from Vinod would change his fortune. But Joshi had always imagined Vinod as an archetypal crazy scientist who will one day die impoverished in spite of carrying out ground-breaking research work because he had no sense of handling or accumulating money. Even if Vinod decided to do the job for Abbasi, he wondered whether he would give him a cut of the money or cut him off completely as he knew very well that he had broken the bond of trust between them.

'You can't buy me! You can't buy my principles!' said Vinod.

Principles! My foot!' Joshi thought. He needed money, to buy his children new toys, to buy a sturdy wood table, to buy a house in Bandra and buy expensive earrings, pendants and diamonds for his wife.

'There's no hurry, Mr Vinod. I'll give you a week's time. Think about it and let me know. Here's my card in case you change your mind,' said Abbasi.

Vinod didn't reply. He got up in a rage, stared at Joshi, and shook his head a bit which meant that Joshi had to follow him without saying a word.

***

Arthur Road Jail had originally been built to accommodate eight hundred prisoners but in a city like Mumbai where the crime rate is very high, the average number of inmates always exceeded its capacity. To solve the issue, the jail administrators decided to shift around 1000 of its 3000 inmates to Taloja Central jail – a 2200-capacity prison in Navi Mumbai which looked like a residential complex built amidst lush green grasses and scenic mountains. The shifting took place on a quiet Sunday. This was the day when the petty thieves with petty crimes met with high-profile thieves with high-profile crimes. And that's when a man imprisoned for dealing cocaine met with a young bike thief, who had been sentenced to six months for stealing bikes from local railway stations. The bike thief had already served six months in Taloja jail and was due for release within the next couple of hours. He assured the cocaine dealer that he would carry a message for him.

On a piece of paper, the cocaine man wrote the name and address of Vinod Johri, and a short note informing him that he was stuck in prison. He gave the note to the bike thief and told him to give his name to Vinod to get some money as reward for delivering the message. Before leaving the prison, the bike thief smiled at the cocaine man, and his eyes spoke of hope as he neatly rolled the note into a small tube and inserted it in one of his ears to hide it from the jail authorities.

***

An eerie Sunday night

It was a full moon night. The stars looked like scattered glass pieces in a black sky. The street dogs were lying down on the sidewalks, their ear flaps in a resting pose, their eyes half-closed, and their rear legs neatly tucked under their bellies. A rustle roused one of the street dogs. It stood with its tail held high and stiff and its ears pointed up. It barked and howled as the bike thief entered Vinod's street. Seeing one street dog howling and barking, the other dogs joined the bark fest, alarming the pot-bellied security guard guarding Vinod's bungalow.

In Vinod's laboratory, there was an uncomfortable silence. A pang of guilt shot through Joshi when he saw Vinod's face. For seven long years Vinod had believed and confided in him but Joshi had broken his trust.

Now Joshi was neither his friend nor his enemy; he was something less than a friend and less than an enemy. Vinod initially thought of doing away with him but seven years of togetherness stopped him from taking such impulsive decisions.

Just then, the laboratory telephone rang.

Vinod took the call himself. It was the pot-bellied security guard on the other side, calling him from the front gate. 'Sir, someone wants to see you.'

'Who is it? Why does he want to see me?'

'He is not giving his name, sir,' said the guard.

'Tell him to come tomorrow,' said Vinod.

'He says he has an urgent message for you, sir.'

Must be one of Abbasi's sidekicks. 'Tell him I am busy,' said Vinod.

'Sir, he says it's really important, it's about your friend.'

Vinod was about to slam the phone down but at the mention of his friend's name, a shade of happiness was seen on his face and his voice now assumed a soothing tone. 'Send him inside,' he said.

The bike thief walked into the laboratory and stared blankly at Vinod. Joshi was standing at a desk. Before the bike thief could say anything, Vinod approached Joshi with the aggression of a tiger nearing a cornered deer and ordered him to leave the lab. Joshi walked out of the lab with a heavy heart.

When asked to sit, the bike thief sat on one of the tall, long-legged wooden stools in the lab and took out a crumpled piece of paper from his front pocket. He unfolded it before handing it to Vinod.

'Your friend wanted me to deliver this message to you,' said the bike thief. Vinod read and re-read the note, his face lined with shock.

'Who are you?' asked Vinod.

'That's not important right now! I am just a messenger. Your friend is in deep shit, you have to save him as soon as possible.'

'What happened? Why is he in jail?' asked Vinod, his voice hoarse.

'He was caught with powder but he seemed innocent to me.'

'Thanks for your help!' said Vinod, and waited for him to leave. Instead, the bike thief blushed and scratched his scalp. Seeing him blush, Vinod understood that he needed something. He thought for a moment and took a wad of currency from his pocket. He counted out thousand rupees and gave it to the bike thief.

'Did he say anything else?' asked Vinod.

'He said it was important for him to get out as quickly as possible. He was talking about going to America for some important assignment,' said the bike thief, stuffing the money in his pocket.

After the bike thief left the lab, Vinod scanned the crumpled note and took in his friend's round handwriting. It reminded him of his college days. Vinod had met Peter in the winter of 1998 in Mumbai University, Fort, near Victoria Terminus. He had given him a pen at the enrolment counter while filling forms for UG courses. Vinod had opted for Physics as his interest was in knowing about nature and Physics actually means *Knowledge of Nature*. And Peter was interested in experiencing it, so he opted for Biology – the science of studying life, which made him experience nature. Vinod liked Peter's way of looking at things, his approach to life and his adventurous nature. They both clicked instantly and became friends.

After completing college they parted ways, and chased their own dreams. Vinod worked hard to become a senior scientist heading the Quantum Physics Department and Peter was busy in setting up his own serpentarium. Though work sucked their time, they somehow managed to keep in touch, and Peter often met Vinod at his Bandra residence.

Vinod couldn't believe that Peter had been arrested for dealing drugs. In their long friendship, he had never even seen him smoke a cigar or down alcohol except for one episode of snorting coke. Safely pocketing the note, Vinod decided to meet Peter at Taloja Central jail.

***

It was almost evening and there was a chill in the air. Vinod warmed himself with a thick overcoat that completely covered his shirt except for the collar which was out, flapping, and looked like a dog's ears. His grey trousers were a perfect match for his white shirt.

A thick-moustached policeman verified Vinod's identity and address. After completing the formalities, Vinod was told to meet the jailor. The jailor asked him about his profession and his relationship with Peter. After probing him for about ten minutes, he called one of the wardens to usher him to Peter.

'Fifteen minutes is what you get, not more than that,' said the jailor.

Vinod entered a small hall lit by a shaft of weak sunlight coming through a small window. There were two chairs and a wooden table. To bring more light and air, the warden pressed a couple of switches that brought a ceiling fan to life and made a bulb glow with yellow light.

Vinod took a chair and was eager to see Peter. He removed his thick overcoat and fanned himself as it was hot inside.

Just then, Peter appeared. His eyelids were puffed and he had circular bruises all over his body. A tall, well-built warden supported Peter and helped him to a chair opposite Vinod.

'You have only fifteen minutes to talk to the accused,' said the warden, looking at his watch.

'For God's sake,' Peter said, 'don't call me the accused.'

A policeman standing near him hit him hard on his back. Peter shouted in pain. Vinod couldn't stand the sight of his best friend writhing in pain. He asked the policeman not to beat Peter and it took a while for things to settle down. He asked for a glass of water and placed it near Peter who lifted it with shaky hands and consumed the water in one go. Peter spoke softly, and Vinod had to lean forward to hear him. He told Vinod that he was innocent. He narrated the events that had led to his arrest and the price he had to pay for being in the wrong place at the wrong time.

Fifteen minutes were over. To Vinod it had felt like fifteen seconds.

'Don't worry, I'll get you out of this place as soon as possible,' said Vinod before leaving.

Peter had to believe Vinod. If at all there was someone who could help him, it was Vinod because Peter had no family. A few years ago, his father and mother had died in a car accident when the car they were in collided with a lorry and burst into flames. He had never made any thick friends except for Vinod. And Sudhir was more like a brother to him.

***

The streets and alleyways of Washington, D.C. are a mix of numbers, letters and geometric shapes. Some streets are called 7th Street, 14th Street; some are called H street, K Street and some are Circles and Squares: Columbus Circle, Garfield Circle and Westmoreland Circle, Franklin Square, Lincoln Square and Union Square. John Anderson stayed on one such numbered street: First Street in NE region of D.C. He lived in a penthouse in an apartment building. Set on a rooftop terrace, the apartment gave John a fine view of the skyline. Each section of his house was furnished with distinctive materials. The windows were high and wide. The rooms were spacious. The floors were made of marble. It had all the amenities that it was supposed to have to lead a luxurious "life on top."

It was holiday season and D.C. was deluged with sparkling lights and holiday merriment. The weather was surprisingly warm and sunny. John sat at a table on his sun-filled balcony and switched on his laptop. It booted with a beep sound and prompted him to enter his credentials. After entering his login credentials, he activated the in-built webcam and opened Skype. He connected to his home Wi-Fi and adjusted the webcam settings to improve the video quality. And after pressing a few buttons, he was all set to initiate a video call with Vinod Johri.

The contents in Vinod's e-mail had drawn him like a magnet. After hearing his speech about depression, Vinod had got in touch with John, and mailed him a note about the Thought

Projector. He assured him that his invention would help psychologists cure patients suffering from depression and other mental illnesses.

John greeted Vinod and spoke in a serious tone of voice. 'Winter in D.C. and in other parts of USA starts in the second week of December. The temperatures are usually very low. And that's when the count of patients suffering from psychological illnesses shoots up. An appointment with a psychologist seems like a distant dream.'

'During the gloomy days of winter, more people suffer from depression. In psychological language it is called SAD – Seasonal Affective Disorder. Patients suffering from SAD struggle with the changing seasons, experience symptoms like fatigue, sadness, loss of interest in activities, sleeping more or less than usual and eating more than usual. For the past twelve years, we at APA have been developing and testing novel therapies to treat SAD but we are not able to make any breakthrough. Diseases that affect the mind are quite different from diseases that affect the organs. That is why it becomes difficult for psychologists to deal with psychological disorders as there is no one-size-fits-all treatment to cure them. People are different and each one has a mind of their own. Though we have not reached a point where we can say we have a cure for depression, researchers are trying their best to find effective treatments to reduce the effect and symptoms. Only a few patients recover despite various antidepressants to choose from. Your TG will help us look through their complex thoughts as depression resides in their thoughts and in their inability to leave the past and construct a better tomorrow.'

Many ideas were exchanged and the video conference lasted for an hour. In that time, John spoke about APA and Vinod spoke more about the TG and its ability to capture and screen recurring thoughts.

Initially, when Vinod had mailed John about his work, as it was coming from an unknown researcher in India, he had viewed it as a possible fraud. But when he had casually asked his colleagues to take a look at Vinod's research papers, they found his research work intriguing, and that was when John believed Vinod and wrote a mail to him, expressing his interest in his work.

***

Joshi was happy and surprised: happy because Vinod had called him to his lab on a Sunday to discuss something important, and surprised because he spoke to him in a pleasant manner over the phone. After the Alibaug incident, Joshi had been ignored by Vinod. And now, all of a sudden when Vinod spoke to him courteously, his heart pounded out of his chest. Vinod's tone left him in a stupor and Joshi knew that Vinod will definitely forgive him.

Carrying a notebook and a pen, Joshi took a taxi to Bandra and reached Vinod's lab. To his surprise, Vinod was waiting for him with a warm smile on his face. When told to come in, Joshi walked in like a latecomer (though he came on time), his head tilted down and his gaze fixed at the mosaic floor. Joshi couldn't meet his eyes. The feeling of guilt was buried deep in his heart and he was not able to get over it.

'Sit down, Joshi.'

'Once again, I am sorry ... sorry for everything,' Joshi said.

Vinod nodded.

'You know, I did this to kick-start our project,' continued Joshi.

'I know, I know,' said Vinod smilingly. 'You shared things that weren't supposed to be shared. You made a mistake. But that's OK.'

'Any luck with the grants?' asked Joshi, diverting his attention from the Alibaug episode. 'No,' replied Vinod. 'No luck. Do you know anything about Abbasi? ... I mean more about him?'

'No,' replied Joshi. 'I know only Ahmed. He's my friend and we studied in the same college.'

Before Vinod could say anything, Joshi continued. 'It was a mistake. I was drunk. I told him about your invention over a couple of drinks. And when he told me that his boss could help us, I was interested in making a deal with them. So, I told him to call you and fix a meeting. My intention was to get things rolling.'

'Is he a good man, this Abbasi?'

'I don't know. Ahmed says, he is into drugs but I don't believe him,' said Joshi.

'Really?'

'Even if he is into drugs, nobody can touch him. He was once a politician, and the Mumbai Police is in his pocket. He has a lot of political links.'

'And you wanted me to make a deal with a liquor baron, who is also a politician and a drug dealer. Liquor! Politics! Drugs! That's a deadly combination,' said Vinod.

'I was just thinking about you, about me, about us, our stalled projects and the funds we need to chase our dreams,' said Joshi. He gathered some courage and continued his speech. 'I don't think we are doing something terrible. In fact, it will help us succeed in our scientific endeavours.'

Vinod sighed.

'I may sound stupid to you but the fact is that we are not empowering him with a machine gun or with a nuclear weapon for him to blow up Mumbai with a click of a button or go about shooting civilians. We are just helping him read people's thoughts which will enable him to make better business deals,' said Joshi.

Vinod sighed again and said, 'It will also enable him to do a hell of a lot of other things. It will give him power! He can strip everyone's thoughts with his penetrating gaze! In the hands of bad people even a needle is a knife!'

'I am not forcing you to sign the deal. I am just stating the facts,' said Joshi.

After discussing the pro and cons of accepting Abbasi's deal for about an hour, Vinod told Joshi, 'Tell Abbasi that I would like to meet him tomorrow.' Those words gave Joshi a ray of hope.

***

The venue was the same, Abbasi's Alibaug bungalow. It was about noon when Vinod and Joshi, escorted by Ahmed, walked into Abbasi's living room. The weather was cloudy and breezy. Abbasi, who had sniffed and snorted cocaine a few minutes back, buried the smell coming from his mouth and nostrils with a mouth freshener and masked the faint kerosene smell that dwelled in the air with a room freshener. He looked animated and welcomed Vinod and Joshi with a beaming smile.

'Wonderful! Nice to see you again,' said Abbasi. 'It's lunchtime, you must be hungry.'

Ahmed ushered them to the dining hall and asked the maid to serve lunch. Abbasi sat at the head of the table with Vinod and Joshi on his right, and Ahmed at the opposite end. The maid brought out their lunch of butter *naan* with spicy *paneer tikka masala* and some rice with *daal*.

'Tell me, Vinod, how long have you been working for Tata Institute of Fundamental Research?' asked Abbasi, stuffing some soft butter *naan* into his mouth.

'It's been more than ten years now,' said Vinod.

'Any luck in resuming your stalled projects?'

'No luck till now.'

'My offer is still on ... If you want to reconsider your decision.'

'On that day I was a bit agitated; after reaching home, I gave it some thought and now I am here to talk business.'

'That's good news!' smiled Abbasi.

'But if you think that I am doing this for money, then you are wrong!' said Vinod.

Abbasi was taken aback for a moment. Ahmed looked at him with suspicion and Joshi appeared confused.

'I am doing this to help my friend,' said Vinod. Abbasi's face brightened like a 100 watt bulb. 'I'll accept your deal on one condition.'

'What is that?' asked Abbasi, leaning towards his side to hear him out.

'I want you to help my friend,' said Vinod.

'Yes, why not? Is he in financial trouble? I am offering you money as a part of our deal.'

'No, he is not in financial trouble,' said Vinod. 'A few days ago, I met him in a place where he is not supposed to be.'

'Where is he?' asked Ahmed.

'In prison.'

'Where?' questioned Abbasi.

'In Taloja Central Jail,' replied Vinod. 'He was arrested for dealing drugs. But I know he is innocent.'

'How can I help him?' asked Abbasi.

'You'll have to do something to get him out of jail.'

'Yes, that's possible,' said Abbasi.

'And you'll have to get him out of jail as soon as possible. It's a time-bound affair.'

'Now that's a challenge!' said Ahmed. 'And what to do if you ditch us after we help your friend?'

'If you can't do this, then I'll have to walk out on this deal.' said Vinod.

'Hey! We'll be able to do this, it's possible! We can get him out,' assured Abbasi.

'Good!' said Vinod. 'Here's the deal, you'll have to get my friend out of jail as soon as possible and after I know that he is out, I'll accept your deal and give Joshi a 100-page manual which will carry step-by-step instructions on how to build and test Thought Glasses. If Joshi works alone, it is going to take 20 days for him to build it himself.'

'Why can't you build it?' asked Abbasi.

'That's not possible,' replied Vinod. 'I am currently working on some important projects and can't be absent from work for such a long time. Also, I don't want anyone to develop even the slimmest suspicion about our true activities. The only way out is to get Joshi involved in the project. And as he reports to me, I can give him 20 days off to work. That will give some anonymity to this project. '

'Why can't you get someone to help him?' questioned Ahmed.

'You want the whole world to know about it, eh?' asked Vinod. 'I want to keep it a secret.'

'But what if I get stuck somewhere?' asked Joshi.

'I'll help you over the phone, don't worry!' said Vinod. 'Or I may visit you once a week to review your progress.'

At the back of Joshi's mind, the thought of why Vinod had delegated such an important project to him was pestering him. He could have very well constructed it all by himself. But at this point in time, accepting the deal mattered more to him than who would do the work.

'Will Joshi work in your lab?' asked Ahmed.

'No. The glasses have to be constructed in total secrecy,' replied Vinod. 'You'll have to find a secluded place and transfer all the necessary lab equipment there for him to work with total concentration.'

'That can be done,' said Abbasi.

'And what if the final product turns out to be laughable; a funny-looking, out-of-the-world glasses! My point is, it should not arouse curiosity when worn. It should look like normal glasses or more like sunglasses,' said Ahmed.

Vinod looked at Ahmed and smiled thinly. 'Though the glasses will have sensors fitted onto its side and be equipped with a tiny projector built into the other side, we will expertly design it to make it look ordinary.'

'I'll give you 40% of the promised amount after you give me a copy of that 100-page manual. Joshi will work under my supervision. After he is done with the project, and if it is seen to be working fine, I'll give you the remaining 60% after successful demonstration,' said Abbasi in a stern voice.

'What about financing my projects?' asked Vinod.

'I remember our deal and I remember what I said before. You can start doing your experiments and I'll take care of the finances,' said Abbasi smilingly. 'Let's get started! Ahmed, get his friend out of jail as soon as possible.'

'What's his name?' asked Ahmed.

Just then, the maid put a steel bowl of hot water with some cut lemons floating on it on the table for Vinod to wash his hands.

'Peter,' said Vinod, dipping his hands in the bowl. 'He's innocent! As I said before, we'll have to get him out of jail as soon as possible.'

'We can get him out of jail easily but getting him out as soon as possible is going to be tough.'

'You'll have to ... ' said Vinod. 'Or else ... '

'We'll get him out, Vinod,' said Abbasi. 'We'll try to get him out within the next three days.'

This assurance brought the deal to a close. The terms and conditions had been clearly communicated from both sides. No one wanted things to go haywire. But from time to time, Joshi sat wondering why such an important assignment had been given to him.

It was evening and the day ended with green *chutney* and *kandha vada* that Ahmed bought from the nearby bakery, and then some cigars.

'Have hot-hot *vada*,' said Ahmed, offering them crispy deep fried *vadas* in a plate with some *chutney*.

Abbasi lit his cigar and started blowing smoke clouds. 'It's celebration time!' said Ahmed and got up to get a bottle of sparkling wine. Vinod had to call him back as it was time for him to leave. It was half past six and Vinod made his apologies, saying he had things to sort out at the lab. Leaving, he shook hands with Abbasi and Ahmed. Joshi followed him as usual like an obedient disciple.

***

After spending a few weeks in the prison, Peter had lost about five kilos. He looked thin and wiry. His body was stamped with red patches caused by the blows that he had received from the wardens. One fine morning, the prison guards walked towards Peter's den and alerted him by hitting the steel prison bar with a *lathi*. It made a shrill metallic sound. Peter got up with a start and stood obediently.

'Come out!' the warden shouted as he opened the cell door. Peter came out. The guards took him to a small office. They waited outside and told Peter to go inside. After entering, Peter saw two men – the prison official and Ahmed.

'You are Peter no?' asked Ahmed.

Peter nodded.

'Please sit down,' said Ahmed.

Peter looked at the prison official and asked, 'May I?' The prison official nodded with half-closed eyes. Following his gesture, Peter sat. His legs were shivering. After making himself comfortable, he stared at Ahmed suspiciously and studied his features. He looked at his glowing gold chain amidst his bushy chest hair, his sparkling gold watch amidst his bushy curly forearm hair and to him Ahmed looked like a bear decked with gold ornaments. A rich bear.

'Who are you?' asked Peter.

'That's an irrelevant question considering the situation at hand. Your friend sent me here,' said Ahmed. 'A very good friend of yours.'

Peter initially gave a puzzled look but soon guessed the friend to be none other than Vinod.

'I am here to get you out,' said Ahmed and looked at the prison official who blushed and coughed.

Peter's eyes went wide and his face brightened. A new energy entered his spine and that made him sit upright.

'One lakh,' said Ahmed, looking at the prison official.

'Not possible, it's a drug case,' said the prison official curtly.

'Two lakhs,' said Ahmed.

'Not possible, things are just not the way they used to be.'

'What the fuck! Have you guys gone nuts? I just got you a new LCD TV last month, and after doing so much all I get to hear from you is NOT POSSIBLE!' said Ahmed.

'I am sorry Ahmed. I can't help you in this case.'

'Why?'

'Drug cases are dealt with by the Anti-Narcotics Cell,' said the official. 'You'll have to speak to the Senior Police Inspector, Mr More.'

Ahmed had already done his homework by scanning the profiles of police officials who worked for the Anti-Narcotics Branch. Headed by DCP (Anti- Narcotics), it initiated action against persons who were involved in illegal sale and possession of Heroin, Hashish, M. Tabs, Methaqualone, Opium, Ganja, Cocaine, Charas, Acetic acid, LSD, Bhang, Morphine and Prezapam Chemicals.

'I know ... I know ... ' said Ahmed. 'I spoke with him this morning. He must be on his way now.'

After ten minutes, Mr More walked into the room and greeted Ahmed with a *namaste*. Seeing him, Ahmed leapt straight to the point. 'I want him out of this jail as soon as possible,' he said, pointing at Peter.

'It is not like before Ahmed,' explained More. 'Things have changed.'

'What the fuck has changed?' exclaimed Ahmed.

Inspector More took out a four-month-old newspaper cutting from his front pocket and showed it to Ahmed.

Senior Inspector Murali Rao was appointed the new Assistant Commissioner of Police, Anti-Narcotics Cell, Mumbai. After taking charge as the city's Police Commissioner, Mr Rao told reporters, 'It's really a dream come true for a young lad from Kurla slums to become Mumbai's Commissioner of Police.'

'So what's the big deal? I'll buy him too!' said Ahmed, scanning the news clipping.

'That's not possible,' said Inspector More. 'He is very strict and brutally honest.'

'I'll talk to him in a language everyone understands – money!' said Ahmed.

'I am cautioning you, Ahmed! Don't play with him. He'll rip you off ... ' warned Inspector More. 'Following a tip-off from a telephone call, Inspector Rao rushed to the spot and had caught this fella red-handed with powder. Even I was there when he got arrested. He's not going to leave this bloke until he cracks the case. As a friend, I'd advise you not to poke your nose into this high-profile case. And you should consider yourself lucky he's not in office right now. Currently, he's unwell but he could be back anytime!'

After hearing about Rao's heroic episodes, Ahmed got up quietly and left the jail without saying another word.

***

Until 2009, Taloja Jail had been just another remote prison on the periphery of the city. But when high-profile gangsters like Daddy and Captain took shelter in Taloja, security was beefed up with CCTV cameras monitoring the corridors and movements in and around the jail. Every movement of the inmates was scrutinized. The double-storeyed *anda* (so called for their circular shape) housed gang lords and drug dons. So, escaping from Taloja seemed a remote possibility for Peter.

One morning, Peter was standing in queue with the other inmates for his breakfast and thinking about his meeting with Ahmed. He was sandwiched between two towering personalities: one a crazy, cruel-hearted thirty-year-old serving a life sentence for murder and the other a cunning, tough, thirty-six-year- old serving fifteen years for crimes of violence. 'Today, you'll have breakfast with us,' said the thirty-six year old. Peter turned back and looked at him. His chin had knife marks. 'Keep walking and sit next to us near the security-force building,' said the life-sentence man.

After getting his breakfast, Peter sat next to them and glanced them with doubtful eyes.

'You want to get out of this hell hole, don't you?

'Ahmed's ... ?' hissed Peter and before he could complete his sentence one of the convicts answered with a soft 'yes.'

'Listen to me carefully,' said the other. 'You cannot escape from this jail. It's impossible! But don't worry! If you act according to our plan, you will breathe fresh air.'

'What am I supposed to do?' asked Peter.

The two convicts briefed him on the plan in hushed voices. Peter's head was filled with questions after hearing the plan.

'What if the prison doctor finds out that I'm faking it?'

'He won't,' replied one of the convicts. 'Don't worry, Ahmed Bhai will take care of him. But try to act like a method artist; it should look real!'

After eating his *chapatti* and drinking his soup, Peter got up slowly, dropped his aluminium plate attracting the prison wardens standing nearby and collapsed to the ground with a thud. He curled himself like a teased earthworm and shouted out in pain. Seeing him in this condition, one of the wardens lifted him with his strong arms and took him to a prison doctor. The doctor examined him and advised the jailor to take him to the nearby hospital for treatment.

Following the doctor's advice, Peter was admitted to Vashi Civic Hospital. He complained of pain in his chest and shortness of breath. The chief doctor at the hospital told the Taloja jail administrators to send some guards to keep an eye on him as Peter had to stay overnight to complete some tests which were scheduled for the next morning.

Two plainclothes officers stood outside Peter's ward to keep a check on him and two uniformed police officers were stationed outside the hospital's main entrance to monitor people walking in and out. Peter was not an ordinary convict. He was a high-profile convict. Late in the evening, Deputy Commissioner of Police, Mr Parkar visited the hospital to check the security measures that were deployed to keep an eye on Peter as he was their only link to sniff and catch the other convicts who had escaped without leaving a trace.

At 12:05 A.M., two well-built guys attacked the uniformed police officers and rendered them unconscious with a single blow. At 12:10 A.M., a black Toyota stood with its engine running at the back of the hospital. At 12:20 A.M., Peter told the nurse that he wanted to go to the bathroom. At 12:30 A.M., the nurse found the plainclothes officers lying motionless on the bench outside Peter's ward. Shocked, the nurse alerted the hospital officials to the situation, and at 12:40 A.M., the officials broke right through the bathroom door and saw a large hole right above the toilet sink and some broken glass pieces scattered around the bathroom. Peter had escaped through the window. When the police investigated the matter, eyewitnesses reported that they had seen a black Toyota near the hospital building, but it sped away like a bullet! And before they could see the number plate, it had been lost from sight.

***

A sudden shower of rain, just after evening twilight, scented the air with a mix of dust and car fumes. Standing near the window of his dining room, Vinod breathed in the petrichor and the smell of Mumbai and felt emotional. He glanced out the window and saw people jostling on a crowded street; he saw a beggar standing and staring aimlessly; somewhere in the distance, he heard the sound of a moving train. And as he was getting sucked into the abyss of Mumbai, he heard someone calling him.

He shook himself out of his reverie and realised that it was his maid calling him for dinner. The table was set with his favourite dishes. A glass jug of water stood on a side table. The maid poured some water for him and served him his favourite food. After she was done with her job, Vinod took out some money and gave it to her. She hesitated and said no to the money but Vinod insisted and told her to take it as an incentive for her loyalty and punctuality. Finally, she took the money and left his house.

Vinod couldn't eat properly. Restlessness swelled in him and made him pace to and fro. His living room was in a mess. In his bedroom, on his bed lay two big American Tourister bags stuffed with clothes and other items.

Just then, the telephone rang.

Vinod answered the call. It was Peter at the other end. His breath was coming in gasps. Vinod told him to calm down.

'I escaped,' said Peter.

'That's great news!'

'Thank you! Thank you so much!'

'Where are you calling from?' asked Vinod.

'From a public telephone booth,' replied Peter.

'Were you able to get in touch with your friend?' asked Vinod.

'I've not called him yet, but I am sure I'll meet him. Thank you! Thank you so much Vinod!' said Peter and before Vinod could say goodbye, Peter disconnected the call.

Abbasi had kept his promise and now it was Vinod's turn to fulfil his wish of finding out what was hidden inside a person's head.

Just then, the telephone rang again. This time, it was Ahmed on the other end.

'We got him out as promised,' said Ahmed. 'But we couldn't do it in a quiet way.'

***

Some of the things needed for the glasses were picked up from Vinod's lab, some of them shifted to an isolated place near Navi Mumbai. After following Vinod's instructions, the isolated place was transformed into a well-equipped lab, ready to pull the lever and kick-start the ambitious project. Abbasi invited Vinod and Joshi to the lab to discuss the deal.

The meeting room adjacent to the lab was set up with a big conference table flanked by chairs. Vinod and Joshi sat next to each other on one side of the table while Abbasi and Ahmed sat on the other side, facing them. Joshi saw Ahmed holding a big black briefcase on his lap. Refreshments were brought to the table: hot *samosas* and masala tea. Ahmed grinned at Vinod and boasted about the efforts that had got Peter out of Taloja jail. There was tension and excitement in the air. Joshi couldn't sit still. For the sake of doing something, he grabbed a *samosa*, took a bite and held it mid-air as Vinod placed a 100-page manual on the table. He pushed it towards Abbasi. It looked like a hardbound book and was titled *Instructions to build and test TG*. Under the title was Vinod's name: Vinod Johri, Senior Scientist, Quantum Physics Department. Abbasi took the book, turned a few pages and read a few lines.

A mind-reading machine or glasses when built with precision can successfully decode electrical brain signals. An invisible beam can penetrate the brain, strike the brain matter and study the neurons. A small decoder analyses the beam which travels back after studying the grey matter. The beam carries information about brain regions that light up as blobs when a person thinks about a particular image or event. It also captures images on the retina and couples it with brain signals to deduce thought patterns. To analyse patterns, the brain should be segmented into little boxes called Voxels. Information in the form of voxel patterns can be stored in a chip with a storage space of 1 TB (Terabyte). Once the chip stores enough samples, the decoder can start to deduce what the person is actually looking at or thinking about. The voxel patterns can also be copied on to a computer and stored for future reference.

Abbasi was not able to understand anything. He called Joshi to his side to make him simplify things.

You cannot decode people's thoughts on the first go. You'll have to meet them at least twice to let the beam study their retina and brain regions and store Voxel patterns in a database. After studying the brain functions of the target, the decoder can easily deduce what the target is looking at or thinking about or intending to do by studying the patterns and converting the data into an image. These images are then sent to a tiny projector. The projector will play these moving images like a video and one can instantly see what the target is thinking!

The invisible beam will originate from the right-hand side of the frame near the temple. When it comes back after hitting the target, it goes to the decoder on the left-hand side of the frame near the temple. A small green light indicates that the decoder is ready to interpret thoughts by matching patterns with the help of the database. You'll have to continue meeting your target until you get the green light on the decoder. The tiny projector projects the moving images for you to see behind the glasses. The target has no way of knowing what you are seeing. You'll be equipped with a remote as small as a capsule and with the click of a button you can switch off the video if you want to see the target. It has the capacity to save moving images for you to view later. To put it in simple words, your remote will talk to your glasses and you can switch between views with a click of a button. And you'll be able to see his mind, his memory, his brain and you will be capable of reading him.

Joshi couldn't wait to get his hands on the manual. After reading a few pages, he explained to the Abbasi-Ahmed duo the basic working of the TG. It took Abbasi a while to understand the concept involved.

'Here's your advance, as promised. Hot cash!' said Abbasi, pushing the big briefcase towards Vinod.

Vinod opened the briefcase and saw currency notes printed with Gandhi's face, neatly stacked and strapped.

'I'll visit Joshi once a week to monitor his progress,' said Vinod.

'You guys should work together and finish it as soon as possible,' said Ahmed, looking at Joshi and Vinod.

'That's not possible!' replied Vinod. 'As I have told you, I'll have to kick-start my stalled projects. And I have other important projects to complete.'

'When can I start the project?' asked Joshi, looking at Vinod.

'Tomorrow,' replied Vinod.

***

It was a cold morning in Washington and John sipped some hot tea. Christmas was just around the corner. To get started with his work, he initiated a video call from his laptop. Sitting in his Washington penthouse, he was taking notes and waiting for Vinod's face to show up on his screen.

John was impressed by Vinod's remarkable knowledge of Theoretical Physics. Though he had no first-hand knowledge of the subject himself, he had replied to Vinod's mail, expressing his interest in his work as some of his close colleagues had been spellbound after reading Vinod's papers. The one thing that mesmerised John was his idea of building and testing a thought-reading apparatus or Thought Glasses. After reading his PDF titled *Thought Glasses*, John had no intention of smothering his genius by not helping him financially.

The video call was not successful, so John opened his chat program and pinged Vinod.

John: Hey! You there?

Vinod: Yeah!

John: I am impressed! Your Thought Glasses are going to start a revolution in the field of psychology!

Vinod: Thank you!

John: Are you ready to fly?

Vinod: Yeah!

John: I'll catch you in New York. We can stay at my guest house and we can proceed with our plan.

Vinod: Yeah! I'll see you in NY.

John: Did I tell you? ... I spoke about your research to my colleagues in Harvard.

Vinod: Oh yes, you told me.

John: I can get you a Postdoctoral position in Harvard ...

Vinod: Thank you! Thank you so much!

John: I'll get you funds or sponsorship awards, and you can work independently or under the supervision of some principal investigators I know.

Vinod: Awesome!

John: Lack of funding shouldn't stop you researching. I'll help you kick-start your projects and in return I need your Thought Glasses!

Vinod: I hope you haven't spoken about them to anyone ...

John: Don't worry! I've kept them a secret. How much time do you need to build it from scratch?

Vinod: I can build them in seven days!

John: That's great! We will test them on patients suffering from psychological disorders.

Vinod: You mean mental disorders?

John: Yes. And do you know this ... the causes of mental disorders are varied and in some cases unclear ...

Vinod: You mean to say there is no single accepted or consistent cause?

John: Yes. And this might interest you... in some cases like depression, the exact cause is unknown. Researchers talk about balance of certain chemicals called neurotransmitters but that's just a theory.

Vinod: I've heard about serotonin...

John: That's a chemical prevalent in certain areas of the brain and it controls mood and emotions.

Vinod: What about antidepressants? How do they function? I remember you saying that they are of no benefit.

John: The bare truth is there is no cure for MDD – Major Depressive Disorder. All we do is, balance the chemicals and reduce the symptoms.

Vinod: That's scary!

John: And these antidepressants affect heart rate and blood pressure. They sometimes make you drowsy.

Vinod: Yeah! I know!

John: So, one wants to know what is going on in their heads ...

Vinod: Thought Glasses will help you ...

John: Yeah! We can also extend its benefits to treat mental disorders.

Vinod: What are the current treatments available?

John: Currently, there is no cure for depression. We just reduce the symptoms by balancing the chemicals in the brain.

Vinod: Oh!

John: And patients suffering from depression, they don't say anything, and they don't share sensitive information. You see ... it's a personal thing!

Vinod: Yeah! You are right! In India, depression is a serious and insidious problem. Studies say 36% of India is depressed and that's only the reported numbers you see ... many people in India don't talk about it. There's a stigma attached to talking about depression. I want to help my country with my invention but corruption is everywhere! Crooked politicians and gluttonous businessmen will end up using my TG in a wrong way! They are only interested in making money and that's why we have few research institutes in India. By the way, what's the final outcome of depression?

John: Final outcome of severe depression is suicide.

Vinod: And suicide statistics are alarming.

John: To tell you the truth, medical treatments for depression have failed miserably ...

Vinod: What about psychological treatments? What about meditation?

John: Learning a type of meditation called "mindfulness meditation" teaches people to focus on the present moment and helps them to stop their mind wandering off into thoughts about the past or the future ...

Vinod: Lord Buddha spoke about this ... that was like centuries back.

John: Yeah! But the most effective treatment for depression is CBT.

Vinod: CBT?

John: Cognitive behaviour therapy. It is a structured psychological treatment which helps in finding out a person's way of thinking and acting. In CBT, the patient works with a therapist to identify patterns of thoughts and behaviour. The aim here is to find out what's making them more likely to become depressed, or stopping them to come out of it once they become depressed.

Vinod: Here's where TG will help you ... It can unlock the mysteries of the mind! You can also study the thought patterns of all depressed patients using TG and derive interesting conclusions.

John: Exactly!

Vinod: What's the role of a psychotherapist?

John: They give pep talks to patients and it takes a psychotherapist months, even years, to build a relationship with the patients. The relationship is then used to explore the patients' past in great depth and find out how these have led to the current depression.

Vinod: Years! That's too long …

John: Yes! With TG, we can see their past, present and what they think about their future instantly! Just like seeing a movie. And I can also use it to treat other complex mental disorders.

Vinod: Yeah! But you'll have to give it some time to collect data.

John: Yeah! I know! Trust me TG is going to create a revolution in the field of psychology and brain science! It's a known fact that depression is a state in which people lose their ability to construct the future. They don't anticipate anything other than gloom and they don't care about tomorrow.

Vinod: We can make the patients wear TG, turn the beam inwards, record their thoughts, find out what's really bothering them, their likes, dislikes and then you can help them construct their future!

John: You are right! I am anxiously awaiting your arrival!

***

On the second day of Joshi's work on TG, Vinod paid a visit to the laboratory. Joshi was wearing his usual lab coat and reading the instructions manual at a feverish pace. He spent the next half hour posing queries and doubts to Vinod. A good four hours of insightful discussion helped Joshi start his work with confidence.

After some time, Ahmed came in to watch the proceedings. He sat in a chair close to them, trying to understand what they were discussing. Everything they spoke about went over Ahmed's head but that was okay as his job was to report to Abbasi about Vinod's involvement in the project and Joshi's progress in constructing the thought-reading device.

On the ninth day of the project, Joshi telephoned Vinod. With the receiver glued to his ear, he waited for Vinod to pick up the call. No one answered. Then he tried his cell phone, but it was switched off. He got back to his work and after half an hour he tried calling Vinod again, but the call went unanswered. He was alarmed and immediately called Ahmed.

Whistling softly to himself, Ahmed was bathing in his Jacuzzi. His cell phone vibrated and sang an old Hindi song with a shrill voice. Sensing the importance of the call, he ran for his cell phone with water still dripping from his body, knowing it had to be Joshi.

'Hello' said Joshi, in a shaky, nervous voice.

'Tell me,' said Ahmed.

'Vinod is not picking up calls,' said Joshi.

'Did you try his cell phone?' questioned Ahmed.

'Yes. It's switched off,' said Joshi. 'And the last time I spoke to him over the phone was ... hmmm ... yesterday evening.'

'Oh! That's more than 24 hours,' said Ahmed.

'Can you drive to his Bandra house and see if everything is all right?'

'I'll do that,' said Ahmed.

Ahmed dried himself and hurriedly wore a white T-shirt with blue jeans. He took his bike and drove to Bandra. When he got to Vinod's place he telephoned him but no one answered, so he waited near the entrance until a security guard came and tapped him from behind.

'What you want?' asked the guard.

'I want to see Vinod. Is he home?' questioned Ahmed.

'He's not here,' said the security guard.

'What do you mean?'

'Can't you see ... ' the guard shouted. 'Can't you see the lock?'

Ahmed blinked twice and peered at the front door through the gap in the main gate. The door was locked and all the windows closed.

'Fuck!' exclaimed Ahmed. He immediately called Abbasi and said, 'We've been fooled by Vinod! He's not at his place! I think he has played a dirty trick on us.'

***

It was supposed to be a bit dark outside the airport, but the tall, new air traffic control tower stood like a blazing torch illuminating the scene. Numerous head- and tail-lights injected liveliness into the nightlife of the city. A network of street lights spread across the length and breadth of Mumbai brightened the city, adding to the oft-repeated phrase: Mumbai never sleeps.

There was a sense of excitement in the air as the world was bidding farewell to the old year and gearing up to welcome the new. The year 2016 was just a few hours away, and around half of Mumbai's population was welcoming it by dancing and singing under electrifying disco lights in a drunken haze. Migrants desperate to get to their hometowns were clogging the departure points: the airport, railway stations, bus stops and taxi stands. Outside the airport, dazzling fireworks decorated the dark sky with stunning colours. And inside the airport, the overall mood was upbeat.

Chhatrapati Shivaji International Airport was crowded and one could hear the constant chatter of people, the ringing of cell phones and the boarding announcements alerting passengers of the departure of their flights. High-quality duty-free merchandise in charming boutiques lured foreigners by offering great discounts. Many travellers were whiling away their time by catching up with friends on Twitter or Facebook on their laptop computers using free Wi-Fi hotspots. Mobile phones were beeping and vibrating with New Year messages. News footage was running on televisions. One screen showed a huge asteroid and the text scrolling across the screen read: *Giant asteroid 1H8876D30 from deep space will strike Earth around December 2020. It is going to form a big crater on the earth's surface.* Another screen talked about a sudden volcanic eruption in Iceland and flashed a message saying, *Hot volcanoes in a cold country!*

Abhishek Patil straightened his tie in the colours of the Indian flag and tied his shoestrings. He was well groomed; his shirt and trousers were clean and pressed to perfection. His attire was in accordance with the grooming policies of Air India for pilots, and his face was etched with a pilot's wisdom. He walked through the security check-in with a smile on his face and adjusted his overcoat before speaking briefly to one of the air hostesses accompanying him. 'I am going to complete 20,000 flying hours soon,' he remarked. His voice brimmed with arrogance and pride.

Ten minutes later, a high-pitched voice emerged from the flight announcement system. *This is the pre-boarding announcement for flight AI 605 to New York. We are now inviting those passengers with small children, and any passengers requiring special assistance, to begin boarding at this time. Please have your boarding pass and identification ready. Regular boarding will begin in approximately twenty minutes' time. Thank you.*

Boeing 777-300, the metallic marvel, was standing at the gate. Patil spoke to the flight attendant about the weather conditions and ride reports. 'Everything is okay sir, we are good to go,' she said. 'Tell Rakesh to do the walk-around,' said Patil, and went to grab a cup of coffee from the terminal before setting up his side of the cockpit.

Rakesh Mehra was the first officer on flight AI 605 and had been Patil's second-in-command for almost two years. He was the flying pilot, though Captain Patil was responsible for the aircraft, its passengers and the crew. Being a long-haul flight, Jatin Doshi had been added to the crew as a relief pilot to assist Rakesh during his rest periods.

As instructed by the captain, Rakesh took a stroll and inspected the overall condition of the aircraft, checking the tire pressure, the status of the oxygen bottles in the cockpit, the wear on the brakes, the engine fan blades for any nicks, and finally eyed the entire airplane for fuel, oil or hydraulic leaks.

Suddenly, a hasty voice emerged from the flight announcement system. *This is the final boarding call for passengers Sudhir Shivaram, Murali Rao, Vandana Rao, Vinod Johri and Ram Johal on flight AI 605 to New York. Please proceed to Gate no. 3 immediately. The final checks are being completed and the captain will order for the doors of the aircraft to close in approximately ten minutes' time. I repeat. This is the final boarding call for Sudhir Shivaram, Murali Rao, Vandana Rao, Vinod Johri and Ram Johal booked on flight AI 605 to New York. Thank you.*

After hearing the announcement, Vinod walked towards the gate in a hurried manner. His heart was pounding with fear. Nervousness stopped him from thinking clearly, and it made him show up late at the airport.

Meanwhile, in the cockpit, Patil and Rakesh tested their oxygen masks and inspected all the electrical circuit breakers to make sure they were in place. Engine fire detection systems were tested resulting in a bell sound that one might usually hear while boarding the airplane. Rakesh checked everything meticulously: Auxiliary fuel pump – Off, Flight controls – Free and correct, Instruments and Radios – checked and set, Landing gear position lights – Checked, Altimeter – Set, Directional gyro – Set, Fuel gauges – Checked, Trim – Set, Propeller – Exercise, Magnetos – Checked, Engine idle – Checked, Flaps – As required, Seat belts/shoulder harnesses – Fastened, Parking brake – Off, Doors and windows – Locked.

'Sir, we are good to go,' he said to Captain Patil and recited a lengthy, boring pre-flight announcement like a school kid who'd been told to recite multiplication tables. *Ladies and gentleman, welcome onboard Flight AI 605 with non- stop service from Mumbai to New York. We are currently fourth in line for take-off and are expected to be in the air in approximately ten minutes' time. We ask that you fasten your seatbelts at this time and secure all baggage underneath your seat or in the overhead compartments. We also ask that your seats and table trays remain in the upright position for take-off. Please turn off all personal electronic devices, including laptops and cell phones or set your electronic devices to airplane mode until an announcement is made upon arrival. Smoking is not allowed on board, including in the lavatories. Also, use of electronic cigarettes is not allowed. Tampering with, disabling or destroying the smoke detectors in the lavatories is prohibited by law.*

One of the air hostesses signalled to the other flight attendants to stand in their respective places, equidistant from each other and when they were ready to enact her words into actions, she addressed the passengers on safety measures, her voice soft and sweet like a fine wine.

Ladies and gentlemen, on behalf of the crew I ask that you please direct your attention to the monitors above as we review the emergency procedures. There are six emergency exits on this aircraft. Take a minute to locate the exit closest to you. Note that the nearest exit may be behind you. Count the number of rows to this exit.

Vinod adjusted his glasses and peered through them to locate his nearest exit.

In the event of an emergency, please assume the bracing position. Lean forward with your hands on top of your head and your elbows against your thighs. Ensure your feet are flat on the floor. Should the cabin experience sudden pressure loss, stay calm and listen for instructions from the cabin crew. Oxygen masks will drop down from above your seat. Place the mask over your mouth and nose, like this.

He looked at Mumbai for the one last time through the thick, small glass opening and felt emotional.

Pull the strap to tighten it. If you are travelling with children, make sure that your own mask is on first before helping your children. In the unlikely event of an emergency landing and evacuation, leave your carry-on items behind. A life vest is located in a pouch under your seat or between the armrests. When instructed to do so, open the plastic pouch and remove the vest. Slip it over your head. Pass the straps around your waist and adjust at the front. To inflate the vest, pull firmly on the red cord, only when leaving the aircraft. If you need to refill the vest, blow into the mouthpieces.

In his pocket, he was carrying a USB drive that stored a PDF document named *Thought-reading glasses.*

We ask that you make sure that all carry-on luggage is stowed away safely during the flight. While we wait for take-off, please take a moment to review the safety data in the seat pocket in front of you.

The runway was cleared for take-off. Captain Patil spoke into the microphone: *Flight attendants, prepare for take-off please.*

The engine started buzzing; the aircraft began its accelerating run along the runway, and a within few minutes, AI 605 was just a tiny speck in the sky, a blip on the radar. Cruising at an altitude of 20,000 feet, at airspeed of 300 miles per hour, AI 605 was flying above the clouds where the air started to thin and it was also getting smoother. Just then, a voice came cutting through the cabin air trying to get some attention of the passengers on board.

Ladies and gentlemen, the Captain has turned off the Fasten Seat Belt sign, and you may now move around the cabin. However, we always recommend keeping your seat belt fastened while you're seated. You may now turn on your electronic devices such as cell phones, and laptops, but we suggest keeping them on airplane mode.

Vinod undid his seat belt. The man sitting next to him turned on his laptop. The screensaver read: THOUGHT IS YOUR ENEMY.

In a few moments, the flight attendants will be passing through the cabin to offer you hot or cold drinks, as well as a light snack and you can use the monitor in front of you to browse our in-flight entertainment. Now, sit back, relax, and enjoy the flight. Thank you.

The relief pilot, Jatin Doshi, sat near the controls, watching all the glowing buttons and levers in the cockpit.

*****

On the twentieth day of the project, the isolated lab had two visitors: Abbasi and Ahmed, who wanted to see Joshi. Smoking a cigar filled with powder, Abbasi held his gaze on Joshi longer than usual as he fiddled with Vinod's path-breaking invention. Ahmed stood next to Joshi and turned the pages of the manual.

It was a moonless night. The weather outside was cold but Joshi was sweating profusely. His hands shivered as he embedded a tiny sensor and a button into the frame. The button, when pressed, was supposed to emit an invisible beam.

'Do you still think it's gonna work?' asked Ahmed.

Joshi kept mum. The day Vinod vanished into thin air, he had wanted to drop the project but curiosity drove him till the last page of the manual and now, he stood before Abbasi with the TG in his hand and his heart in his mouth.

'He has to make it work,' said Abbasi, and his voice pierced Joshi like a dagger.

Joshi sat down and made Ahmed sit right opposite him. After wearing the Thought Glasses, Joshi pressed a small button. It made a beeping sound. Abbasi exhaled few smoke rings and waited for something to happen.

'Think of something,' said Joshi, looking at Ahmed.

Ahmed sat patiently in front of him for two hours, as if his portrait were being drawn. Joshi tried reading his mind with the glasses. He was supposed to see moving images but nothing happened. He clicked the button for the video to show up but nothing happened. It was clear that Vinod had betrayed him.

'Are you able to see anything?' asked Abbasi. His voice was loud and rough.

'No, I think I need to concentrate,' replied Joshi, wiping beads of sweat from his forehead. All his left eye could see was a kaleidoscope of colours and nothing else. The stare that Abbasi gave him made his blood run cold.

Abbasi couldn't hold his patience any longer. He stubbed his cigar using the edge of the ashtray, stood in front of Joshi and delivered a punch to his face. Before Joshi could recover, he punched him again. Never had he felt punches so hard and nasty. The so-called Thought Glasses he was wearing flew off and tinkled to the floor. It was a bloody show on his face. Red streams of blood were gushing from his nose and his face looked like that of a boxer fighting his tenth round with a cut on his upper lip.

'Make it work! Or I'll kill you!' exclaimed Abbasi.

Joshi's heart skipped a beat. He was about to fall but Ahmed supported his trembling body by holding his shoulders. Abbasi splashed a mug of water on his face to bring him out of his stupor.

'Make it work!' shouted Abbasi.

Joshi couldn't react. Not only could he not speak, he couldn't even move.

'Leave him!' Abbasi ordered Ahmed.

Ahmed obeyed his orders and Joshi stumbled and crashed to the ground and landed hard on his ass. Lighting another cigarette, Abbasi stamped him on his chest. Joshi coughed up more blood. His face now looked like a smashed pumpkin.

'Boss, don't beat him more or he'll die,' said Ahmed.

'You fooled me!' shouted Abbasi and stubbed his cigar on Joshi's forehead.

'I will not leave you until I get my money back … Ahmed, tell your friend to do something to make it work, else he'll be killed!'

***

Story 2

Chapter 2: The Venom Collectors

Peter narrates his story

I will have to move quickly before the sun finds me. I'll have to hide myself to be safe. I can't afford to rest. I can't tell my entire story sitting in one place, you'll have to allow for pauses.

Where should I start? My story starts and ends with Sudhir. And because of Vinod, I'm free!

When I was born, my mother wanted me to become a doctor but I grew up as an adventurer and ended up becoming a venom collector. Some may call it destiny. Some may call it fate, but I call it chance. We sometimes meet a person who walks into our life and changes everything – in my case, that someone turned out to be Sudhir.

I had known him for a long time. My mother introduced him to me when I was eight years old. He was our neighbour and we lived in the same colony – cluster of small apartments. We clicked instantly and became good friends. Fascinated by everything around us, we explored and questioned the workings of nature. Like all children, we roamed carelessly and giggled for no reason.

At the beginning of the summer holidays, we would chalk out plans on how to spend the summer vacation in an adventurous way. Like other kids, we did everything with absolute frivolousness, except for two things: climbing and catching.

Our first climbing experience turned out to be dreadful, as I fractured my arm and Sudhir got his leg broken. Climbing the Gulmohar tree was my idea. Dressed with vermillion flowers, fern-like leaves and sword-like dangling pods, it ensnared us with its stunning beauty, but the weak branches at the top made us fall to the ground with a thud.

After recuperating in a local hospital for about two weeks, we were back in business. Because I was big and had more experience in doing things, I usually spoke with the authority of an elder brother, and Sudhir obeyed me. We climbed the same Gulmohar tree and this time we were successful in collecting three dangling swords each. As time went by, we became experts. During Christmas, we wrapped festive lights around tall trees, and that's when we overcame the fear of heights. Next on our list was mountain climbing, and we started our weekly expedition with beginner-friendly mountains. Graduating from climbing trees to climbing mountains gave us a sense of pride and made us happy.

Sudhir liked trekking on higher altitudes. Mountains fascinated us! We enjoyed the view the mountains gave us when we reached their summit and we could hear the meek noise of civilization from the top and that made us taste freedom! Initially, we did rock climbing and when we upgraded our skills, we did snow and ice climbing. Each expedition made us stronger, gave us new life and prepared us to face the future with renewed determination. As time went by, my interest in mountaineering slowly died, but

Sudhir kept his passion of climbing alive. He occasionally taught mountaineering to interested aspirants at the Nehru Institute of Mountaineering in Uttarakhand.

***

Let's go back to our school days where it all began. My mother spanked me for the first time when I destroyed an ant hill. It was Sudhir who introduced me to the secret world of ants. I remember we were in the garden and we saw an ant trail. Sudhir did a field investigation by crushing some ants to see how they communicated distress and danger when attacked. I was amazed by the way the ants shook hand with their antenna, the way they walked with their backs held high and the speed at which they explored new routes when the old ones were disturbed or blocked by an obstacle.

Squashing the rear part of big black ants was Sudhir's favourite pastime. He would prick their watery backs with a needle to drain the fluid and then he would make them walk like a wounded soldier. To test the power of the ants' pincers, he would expertly lift them by holding their backs, tap their heads a few times until they were flustered and heated and then introduce a thin strip of paper between the pincers to gauge the intensity of their bite. After a few weeks of dealing with ants, I tried to match Sudhir's dexterity in handling them but I failed. One bit me on my index finger. Before I could crush it, other soldier ants from the colony attacked me by splitting themselves into different groups. One group attacked my leg and the other was all over my arms. They swarmed upon me, injecting toxin-rich venom and I turned red. I ran to my mother and showed her the little red bumps on my skin. She warned me not to play with red ants and applied some cream. Blisters followed and when I squeezed them, my mom would say, 'Peter! Don't pop the blisters!' in a rhythmic tone.

Our house in Thane had a big garden that teemed with life. One day, while exploring, Sudhir and I came upon the largest fire ant colony I had ever seen. Sudhir collected some ants in a plastic container. He fished out a magnifying glass from his pocket and explained to me about their morphology by holding the glass close to the container.

'They bite by grasping the skin with their pincers and inject the venom through their sting,' Sudhir said. I was both puzzled and amazed when I saw the pincers. What extraordinary pincers! Pincers that injected acid like venom. I wanted to know more about the venom, its chemical composition and how it reacted with our body. 'Formic acid,' Sudhir replied, showing me a bottle of a colourless clear liquid. That's when I realized that I share a chemical relationship with ants. It was pure chemistry! Under Sudhir's expert guidance I caught ants and kept them in small jars. I gave them names and displayed them like trophies. I played with them and when I got bored I cut them up with a sharp blade, trying to find their internal organs and their venom. I heard that scientists found neurotoxins in their venom. I was astounded by the way the ant bridged its system with mine by stinging and the way the venom reacted with my body as if it had a mind of its own and knew what it had to do with my system. Later, I realized what the ants had taught me. Without speaking a word they enlightened me with a deep philosophical message: I don't have a self and I am a part of this universe.

***

Adolescence gave us wings and courage. We graduated from ants and moved to spiders. After befriending an insect collector and learning some tricks from him, Sudhir brought home a venomous spider in a glass jar. It looked creepy. And even after opening the lid, it lay quiescent inside the jar. 'I put it to sleep using carbon dioxide,' he said and turned the jar upside down to place the spider on a soft cloth. It was a giant Indian ornamental tree spider. Yellow and black stripes decorated its body and it exhibited an intricate fractal-like pattern on the abdomen. Sudhir used a stand with a tong like apparatus to hold the spider and introduced a thin stream of water to rinse the fangs. After rinsing, he did something that terrified me. 'I am going to deliver 12 Volts of electricity to make her spit her venom,' he said and administered an electric shock. After that, what had happened was disgusting. The spider puked and at the same time the venom came out of her fangs. It was colourless and Sudhir milked it by placing a thin glass capillary tube near the fangs.

'You know, this venom can be used to prepare medicine that can cure diseases,' said Sudhir. I was amazed. This goes to prove the old adage: anything in excess is a poison. Sudhir indirectly taught me another adage: you can extract good things from bad things.

***

Things that were terrifying and badass impressed Sudhir. He displayed his venom-filled test tubes like trophies and would later teach Deepak about special snake diets and other techniques to improve venom quality. Sudhir was a college dropout. Although he did a bit of formal learning, most of his knowledge of molecular biology and venom was self-taught. He had a passion for venomous snakes and whenever there was a snake show in Mumbai, he would drag me and make me look at them up close.

One day, he saw in the *Times* that a new snake exhibit was to be inaugurated in the city. It would showcase venomous snakes from Australia, North America, Africa and Asia. We saw rattlesnakes, vipers, cobras and mambas flicking their tongues in thick glass cages. Before I could hear it from the exhibit officials, Sudhir had told me everything about venomous snakes. He had warned me about the mambas saying that they are aggressive snakes with unpredictable behaviour and their venom can kill an adult human within 20 minutes. He also boasted about king cobras, saying that they were damn smart snakes and could learn and adapt like humans. Then we discussed vipers and rattlesnakes and by the time we left the exhibit, we were completely sucked into the world of venomous snakes.

Six years later, we owned a Serpentarium Lab and were called the Venom Collectors. Though I was not good at handling snakes, the name stuck to me as I was always seen with Sudhir. We had a rare collection of poisonous snakes, especially king cobras. Sudhir conducted his own personal observations and gained a lot of insights into their behaviour. He heard hisses more than human voices all his life and he immersed himself in the world of venomous snakes.

***

I thought, in every bad thing there is always something good and it turned out to be true in the case of snake venom.

Sudhir's first catch was a nine-foot-long King Cobra. He was eighteen or nineteen years old at that time and before catching the snake, he practised the art of catching slithering non-venomous snakes that were difficult to handle. I was with him when he caught the nine-footer at a lake in Thane. The first thing that made me feel weak in my knees was when it had held me in its cruel gaze. I tried to look away but I couldn't. It drew me like a magnet. I was standing behind Sudhir and could hear my own heart pounding with fear. My hands were shivering and my legs shaking.

Using a snake hook, Sudhir aimed at the upper third of its body but the snake slithered away. After trying hard, Sudhir was able to place the hook somewhere between a third and halfway down its body. He halted it momentarily and with the help of the hook he was able to take it out of the bushes. He then guided it to an open space and without wasting any time, he applied the age-old technique of catching snakes to good effect - he distracted the snake with one hand and quickly grabbed its tail with the other. To his surprise, the cobra swung around and charged towards him, open-mouthed, with a hissing sound. The hiss was not a loud one. It was a constant low frequency hiss, a hiss that still resonates in my ears and fills my heart with all adjectives of fear. Sudhir moved back and I saw the snake's golden hood change colour when I moved back with my trembling legs.

The cobra stood high enough to stare at him again. Sudhir, still holding its lustrous tail, distracted it with his fingers and when it gave him a few seconds of golden opportunity, he seized it by grabbing it behind the head with the other hand. That shifting of his hand from its tail to its head was lightning fast! The cobra was no more a king in his hands; it looked like a defeated solider.

After perfecting his skills as a snake catcher, Sudhir graduated to the next step and began milking snake venom. He would grab the back of the snake's head with his thumb and index finger and then he would gently press on the venom glands to get the venom out. I did my part in assisting him with a vial covered with a plastic film and Sudhir would push the fangs through the plastic to collect the liquid. To get more venom, Sudhir would push the fangs through the plastic several times. The colour of the venom turned out to be clear and colourless, just like our saliva, like spider's venom or ant's venom.

Sometimes during idle moments of solitude I asked myself, 'Why did I choose to become a snake maniac?' and I asked the same question to Sudhir, but he never replied. With a sad smile he would look at the framed photo of his mom and dad nailed on the wall; framed and nailed and dead.

***

I'd like to go back to my high school days again to narrate an incident. This is one incident that I cannot forget. It was a bright sunny day and people were out in great numbers. I was with Sudhir's family, eating *Misal Pav* at a road-side stall in Bandra. Sudhir's father was a banker. When Sudhir introduced me to him, he smiled and patted me on my shoulders. Six months later, he was dead.

When the pav was brought to us on steel plates, we gorged like hungry hyenas. Something was not alright with Sudhir's father. His face was red and he seemed to be in a lot of pain. Seeing him suffer, we immediately asked for the bill and rushed home. It was late at night. Sudhir's father walked to and fro, restlessly, his shirt drenched in sweat, and when Sudhir's mom asked about his discomfort he shouted saying, 'I am pissed because I am not able to piss.'

We were waiting for him to piss. Every time he went to the bathroom, we followed him and waited outside the door to hear the sound. Nothing happened. All his sweaty efforts were in vain. The clock gonged twelve times and the entire city was snoring. I told Sudhir's mom about a doctor friend who could treat her husband.

'Let's go,' she said.

I got an auto and told the driver to go to the doctor's place. While we were travelling, there was silence that engulfed us with melancholy. I broke the silence with a very soft conclusion about his health, using the little knowledge that I had of organs in the human body.

'I guess there's something wrong with his kidney,' I said, and it turned out to be true.

We reached the doctor's place and knocked on the door. A small girl opened it. We walked inside in a hurried manner and briefed the doctor on Sudhir's father's condition. Sudhir's mom sat in a chair in the hall, and Sudhir waited with her. I went with Sudhir's dad to another room where the doctor injected him with some liquid.

'Don't worry, you'll soon feel better,' the doctor said.

In the morning, after much struggle, he finally urinated. His face was etched with relief and satisfaction. He closed his eyes to feel the pleasure of the pale yellow fluid leaving his bladder. An instant later his face crinkled and the pale yellow colour of his urine turned to a deadly red, and he began to whimper. We all rushed to the bathroom and were shocked to find the white of the toilet smeared with thick blood. Sudhir's mother immediately phoned the doctor and after conducting some check-ups, she was told to consult a urologist.

***

In the doctor's waiting room, I was sitting next to Sudhir's father and Sudhir sat between me and his mother. One by one, men with various conditions went into the doctor's room. After thirty minutes of waiting, we were called inside and I sat facing Dr Pai, at his consulting desk, and Sudhir's father sat next to him on a revolving chair. There was a chart on the wall showing a cross-section of a kidney and the path of urine. I looked at it for a moment, and then diverted my attention to Dr Pai.

'You drink alcohol?' the doctor asked Sudhir's father.

'No.'

'You smoke?'

'No.'

'You take drugs?'

'No.'

'You eat pan or gutka?'

'No.'

'Any other bad habits?'

'No.'

'We'll have to scan your kidneys.'

The next day, I got a call from Sudhir. 'He has a tumor in one kidney,' said Sudhir in a broken voice and began to sob. The scans had revealed that the tumor covered his entire kidney and had even become a part of it. Surgery was the only option. The word "surgery" petrified us, and made us weak. Kidney removal was no joke. Several questions started popping like bubbles inside my brain. How could someone live with just one kidney? If they could, then why had the creator installed two kidneys? May be because they act like a filter; a sophisticated waste disposal machinery which deals with junk 24 hours a day, 7 days a week and is susceptible to infection.

Then I thought about Sudhir's family; I thought about operation charges. They were running short of money and Sudhir's father had recently purchased a new 1 BHK flat in Thane by taking a 30-year home loan. The surgery date had to be postponed as Sudhir's mother couldn't arrange sufficient funds. We collected funds from every possible source to remove his kidney but it was not sufficient, so Sudhir's mother sold her gold wedding ring and bangles to arrange for the rest. The surgery date was fixed and the doctor operated on Sudhir's father for four long hours.

I saw his soggy bean-shaped kidney kept in a big glass jar. It looked greater than its normal size as the tumor had covered his kidney like a sheath, like a tortoise shell, and it was popping out from every possible place. Sudhir's mother fainted after seeing it. And after she regained her consciousness, the doctor told her something that made her faint again.

'We'll have to examine his kidney tissue for cancer cells,' the doctor said.

Before taking his soggy kidney to the pathologist, the hospital caretaker stored it inside a jar in a chilled preservation solution and to me it looked like a deep sea aquatic animal. I went along with the caretaker to meet the pathologist.

'We'll examine whether the tumor is cancerous or not,' the pathologist said.

A sample of the tissue was removed from the kidney and examined under a microscope for insight into possible cancerous cells. The results were out the next day.

'The tumor is benign. It is a harmless noncancerous growth. But we will have to monitor him carefully as noncancerous tumors can turn cancerous at a later time. As of now, there's nothing to worry about,' the doctor said.

After hearing the good news, Sudhir's mother heaved a sigh of relief. And after three weeks, Sudhir's father was discharged from the hospital.

***

For five months, Sudhir's father lived with one kidney without any problem. Doctors spoke words of encouragement and told him that some people are born with one kidney and lead normal, healthy lives. Things seemed to be returning to normal, but it was only for a short while. Sudhir's father soon started coughing up blood again. Frequent visits to the doctor and severe abdominal pain made him tired and weary. New symptoms took over his body like an army of soldiers taking over an enemy fortress. The skin of his lips turned bluish. He experienced frequent joint pains that arrested his ability to move. Fever and chills interrupted his sleep cycle. Queasiness kept him awake through the night. Serious symptoms like hallucinations and delusions indicated that he was suffering from a life-threatening condition. Doctors checked him thoroughly. Blood samples were taken, and after two days the test results were out.

'Blood cancer,' the doctor said in an emotionless voice after examining his blood.

We were shocked! Whilst pondering on the question of how this had happened, the doctor briefed us on the possibility of some hidden cancer cells slipping into his blood stream during the operation. His immune system couldn't kill them. To start with, the cancer cells affected his lungs and then attacked his liver and within a few days, they had taken over his entire body. As a last resort, we called a famous Siddha doctor and tried Siddha medicine, but it didn't have any effect. After a lot of suffering, Sudhir's father died.

***

Let's put bad things behind us and talk about some good things. We desperately needed some funds to do the marketing of our Serpentarium and Vinod helped me with some contacts to promote the business. Our Serpentarium was a runaway hit! I was praised for being in the right place at the right time. Everything went nice and easy. But when things get to their extreme, they turn into their opposite. Soon I was cursing myself for being in the wrong place at the wrong time. Because of my inquisitiveness, I ended up in Arthur Road jail. Three weeks before the Arthur Road incident, I received a call from a guy who sounded so academic that I was excited to meet him when he suggested meeting at the Cafe Coffee Day on RK Shirodkar Marg near Parel. When I asked him about the agenda, he heaped praise on me for successfully running a mid-size Serpentarium in Thane and said he wanted to discuss something important. I dressed in fine clothes as his voice seemed to indicate business, and when I entered the coffee shop, I saw him sitting alone with a cup of hot cappuccino at the table near the entrance with an intellectual look etched on his face. He was the only person there.

'Peter?'

I nodded and sat down.

'I am Deepak Malekar,' he said.

He was in his mid-forties and had a big broad nose that looked like a capsicum. With his thick glasses and bald head (and hair in his ears) he looked like a research scholar. After our initial conversation, my guess turned out to be true; he was indeed a research scholar. Choosing a place near Parel for our rendezvous was convenient for him as Haffkine Institute was just a stone's throw from the deserted coffee outlet. Named after Russian scientist Waldemar Mordecai Haffkine, whose research on the anti-plague vaccine saved many lives during the 1896 epidemic in Bombay and Pune, Haffkine is one of the oldest biomedical research institutes in India.

'I am the Head of the Biochemistry department,' he said.

When asked about his job, he spoke about the research projects under his supervision, which when executed successfully, could help create drug formulations that could be used for prevention and treatment of complex diseases like diabetes and cancer.

'I learned about your Serpentarium from one of my colleagues,' he said.

Running our Serpentarium as a tourist attraction was not our ultimate goal though we did it for a while to make some money. We nurtured hissing snakes and milked their venom for medical and scientific research. Ours was a 9000 square foot, four-storey building that housed a total of 19 species of Indian snakes, including 10 species of cobra, 4 species of vipers and 5 species of Indian krait. After Sudhir's father's demise, Sudhir's mom got his bank job and that gave us some financial motivation. She helped us with the bank loan, and with that money, we bought a plot of land and started construction on the Serpentarium. We caught snakes, primarily cobras, and housed them in built-in display cages equipped with secure locks. Sudhir did the handling and catching and I helped him with the paperwork by obtaining Collecting Permits. As snake collectors, it is mandatory to obtain Collecting Permits before bringing snakes into the Serpentarium.

'I heard from my colleagues that your friend is an expert at catching snakes. Is it true?' he asked.

My reply to him was a "yes" with a beaming smile on my face. I understood that he had made a thorough background check on us. Sudhir was indeed an expert at handling and catching snakes. Seeing him in action was like seeing a ballet dancer move; the way he moved his hands and wrists with absolute precision, the speed at which he grabbed the snake's head from behind, and the way he slid his fingers over their slender, colourful, patterned bodies with classiness and finesse was definitely a treat. By 2015, our Serpentarium housed more than 500 venomous snakes in 450 cages, and it became a famous local attraction.

In his 15 years of dealing with snakes, he never got bit even once. Sudhir never believed in Mithridatism – a practice of shielding oneself against a poison by gradually self-administrating small doses of the same to build up immunity. Many of his fellow snake handlers injected themselves with non-lethal doses of venom. Immunizing themselves gave them the edge and boosted their self-confidence while dealing closely with venomous snakes. And to add some fuel to this freaky practice, we once met a guy from Myanmar who had tattooed himself with snake venom to develop immunity.

The Biochemistry researcher leaned back in his seat and asked about Sudhir. 'Where is he?'

'He's in Uttarakhand.'

'What is he doing up there?'

'He teaches there.'

Sudhir taught Basic and Advanced Mountaineering courses to young and aspiring mountaineers at the Nehru Institute of Mountaineering. Located in Uttarakhand amidst a dense pine forest, NIM is rated one of the best mountaineering institutes in India. Sudhir was always excited to go there and he usually made two trips a year and each trip lasted for a couple of weeks. NIM paid him well and that had helped us pay off a portion of the bank loan. More than the loan, paying the interest on the loan sucked our energies and burdened our backs like unwanted luggage. After setting up our Serpentarium, we charged an entry fee from the visitors to show them our amazing collection of snakes. And in the evening, we resorted to snake shows to get more money. Sudhir would take the snakes from the snake bag, put it on the table for the audience to see from a safe distance, and then tame the agitated snake, catch its head from behind, and finally milk it. And I did the marketing part to get more audience for the snake show.

After 30 minutes of casual conversation, the biochemistry researcher touched upon the topic of venomics and we talked about proteins, polypeptides, enzymes and the other ingredients of snake venom. Then, finally, after much deliberation, he spoke to me about his current research project. And the tone of his voice while talking about it made it sound like some secretive task that was being carried out in an undisclosed location.

'VEN40,' he said. His voice was so soft and low that I had to lean forward to hear him.

'What?'

'VEN40, that's the name of the project.'

'VEN40? Is that a secret code or something?' I asked out of curiosity.

He chuckled at my inquisitiveness, as if VEN40 were a well-known acronym.

'VEN stands for Venomics and 40 stands for the number of resources currently working on this project. And 40 is my lucky number too!' he said.

VEN40 was all about exploiting snake venom for the development of novel therapeutics, but turning venom into a trove of useful molecules was no joke. It demanded serious work. I probed him with a lot of questions about the project as the details that he gave me sounded very generic. From his face I could figure out that he was not ready to delve into the details of his current research project over a cup of cappuccino.

'Come to my lab,' he said. 'I have an offer for you.'

Offer! That got me excited. We shook hands and he gave me his card. 'See you real soon, Peter,' he said and left.

***

A Haffkine security guard who looked as thin as a rake stood outside the main entrance of the institute. He did his usual security check after I passed through the screening point. Inside the institute, on the second floor, I saw a room secured with a fire proof door and a two-factor authentication biometric device installed on the wall. They gave me an access card and stored my thumb impression on the computer.

'We'll need a photocopy of your identity proof,' said Deepak. Surprisingly, his face was brimming with glee and I wondered how he had managed to shed his sober academic look.

'Here's my driver's licence,' I said, taking it out of my wallet.

'We take a lot of precautions at a place like this, with all these venomous snakes around,' he said.

The security at the desk gave me back my driver's licence and Deepak ushered me into his facility. We pushed through a door that said 'Authorised personnel only,' and I felt surreptitious as I entered the room. This part of the institute was like a secret underworld space.

A fridge in the corner was filled with tiny bottles of dry snake venom. After scanning all the equipment installed in the facility it took no time for me to realize that I was standing inside a secured hi-tech snake farm. I saw several snake-boxes and rodents confined in small, barren laboratory cages.

'You feed them rodents every week?' I asked.

'Yes,' he said. Then he pointed at a hissing cobra and said, 'This one eats one mouse at one feeding per week.'

'It is generally advisable to breed rats in the snake farm but in our Serpentarium we feed them small chickens,' I said.

On the table next to the rodent enclosure were some pieces of cleaning equipment, latex membrane and miscellaneous items; on top of the big refrigerator I saw some sophisticated electrical equipment.

'You milk them using electrical stimulation?' I enquired.

'Yes. You and Sudhir do it manually I suppose.'

Milking venom through electrical stimulation causes the muscles around the venom glands to contract, forcing the snake to spit venom into the container. Initially, Sudhir used electrical stimulation on spiders and snakes but later he changed his mind as he observed that using small electric currents affected snakes and altered their behaviour.

'We do it manually,' I confirmed. 'Sudhir says, using current has direct physiological effects on them and I believe it too.'

Deepak rubbished my claim and lectured me on the benefits of the electrical method.

'On an average, eight out of ten snake handlers die. The manual method is not safe whereas milking through electrical simulation is safe.'

'So what's VEN40 all about?' I asked. 'New drugs?'

'Yes,' he said, and directed me to a room at the end of the big hall. We walked inside wearing protective masks.

'Here's where we freeze-dry the venom and turn it into powder.'

Having handled sales and marketing activities, I was interested in the conversion rate of liquid venom to dry venom. I probed him for details and he replied promptly like an obedient student reciting multiplication tables.

'One milking produces about 90 to 100 mg of liquid venom, which in turn produces about 10 mg of dry venom,' he said. 'But we are not here to sell antivenins; we are here to study their potential therapeutic properties.'

I sensed an ounce of arrogance and pride in his voice when he said those words. I was waiting for him to get to the point but he continued talking about venom and its ingredients. He spoke in detail about venomics but the conversation turned out to be one-sided as it was too technical for me to respond. The jargon that he was throwing at me escaped me completely but he got my attention back when he talked about a guy who had been completely cured of cancer with the help of drugs made out of snake venom. He told me about a protein called contortrostatin, which had the ability to paralyze cancer cells.

'It disrupts the communication of cancer cells and confines them, allowing us to kill them with chemo and medicine. As far as contortrostatin is concerned, we are yet to move beyond lab rats, and preparing it is appallingly expensive,' said Deepak.

We walked into another room, this one full of cobras, hissing behind secured cages. Each cage was equipped with under-tank heating pads on one end to provide the snake with temperature options like warm and cool. High-tech temperature control sensors were installed, and to me the place looked like a sophisticated quarantine laboratory: it was crowded with small tables kept next to each cage and each table was cluttered with equipment such as snake sticks, snake forks, tongs, snake bags, water bowl and dish, hide box, some collecting vials, a snake egg container and all sorts of other things.

'So what exactly is happening here?' I asked.

'We are breeding different species of cobras in a controlled environment,' he said.

'Why only cobras? Why not other snakes?'

'Because they are special,' he said, and gave a lengthy lecture on the uniqueness of king cobra venom.

'We consider king cobras and other species of cobras to be unique not because of superstitions woven around them but because of the concoction of unique proteins in their venom. We breed them, milk them and study their venom for medical cures. And the use of cobra venom in medicine is not something new; it dates back to the 18th century. The Chinese used cobra venom to treat opium addiction and Indians used it to treat pain.'

His lecture on venom chemistry mingled with the hissing sound of cobras as if they were giving backing vocals to a rap song. I leaned forward to hear him through the noise.

'Cobra venom is one of the fastest-acting snake venom in the world and king cobra venom has so many mysteries hidden within. Every time you milk a king cobra, you are bound to see something new in its venom. It is a complex soup of biological molecules that can change composition, and that's the reason scientists have been studying it for over 50 years and are still not finished with it. They are still identifying new compounds.'

This fact startled me. I had an urge to share this interesting piece of information with Sudhir, but getting him on a call while he was in Uttarakhand was next to impossible.

'Why are these cobras hissing?' I asked him. Cobras are usually shy creatures and they avoid any sort of confrontation. They rear and extend their hood with a hissing sound only if they are continuously provoked.

'They're on a special diet and their altered behaviour is nothing but a side effect. We pick them up from different countries such as India, Myanmar, Thailand, Philippines and South Africa, and breed them here in our facility, milk them and classify their venom based on the environment they belong to before conducting more experiments on them.'

'What sort of experiments do you conduct?' I asked him and he gave me a long drawn out speech.

'Cobra venom primarily consists of neurotoxins which affect the nervous system. Like other venomous snakes, their venom is a toxic cocktail of proteins and polypeptides with a dash of other exotic compounds which have inimitable pharmacological properties. The venom of a Burmese cobra will be different from that of an Indian cobra, as change in the environment alters their venom composition.'

'Wow! I didn't know that.'

'To mimic climatic or seasonal changes we change the temperature in each cage by slowly increasing or decreasing it until a temperature of about 60°F to 65°F is reached. Then we milk them and study their venom composition to see if they have produced any new compounds. Sometimes, we change the snake's diet to see if it has some effect on their ability to produce new biological molecules. We do this by converting some into rat-eaters in spite of them being natural snake-eaters. Sometimes, we feed them a special protein diet with the help of a pump.'

'That's great! So to sum up: VEN40 is an ambitious experiment to find new compounds, or rather a probabilistic approach to see if the permutation and combination of factors such as environment, climate and a snake's diet has an effect on their venom composition. Am I right?'

'Yes, you are right.' said Deepak with a curvy smile.

'So how do we fit in here?'

'You'll help us by catching snakes and supplying venom.'

'Are you kidding? Any local guy can do that for you.'

'I considered my options carefully before letting you visit my facility. I am in immediate need of some Malaysian king cobras; they are touted to be the king of all king cobras and I know that you have half-a-dozen long, slithering, Malaysian cobras in your Serpentarium. I need them for my research.'

'Sure! I'll give them to you.'

'Some cobras prefer to live at high altitudes. Sudhir being a mountaineer and an expert snake catcher can do this job for me very easily. I visited your Serpentarium a few weeks ago and was impressed by your collection of venomous snakes. You have the right mix that I need for my research. And you guys have handled more than 500 snakes, and, believe me, that's a whopping number! I need someone who can understand cobras and Sudhir fits the bill perfectly,' he said, his voice filled with enthusiasm.

Deepak was right. Sudhir knew a lot about king cobras. Everybody used to call him a "snake scientist." Some people well versed in science used to call him a herpetologist but he was more of an ophidiologist – an individual who studies snakes.

'We'll be more than glad to help you,' I said.

'That's great! I'll show my gratitude monetarily and through being a part of VEN40, you'll get to handle venomous snakes from all over the world.'

'Who is funding this project?' I asked.

'The New York Academy of Sciences. They are also doing something similar. They deal with Black Mambas, copperheads and rattlesnakes. They call us every month to get updates. This project is time-bound and constrained by hard deadlines. They need something concrete by the end of this year.'

'Sudhir will be back in two weeks. I'll definitely speak to him about VEN40.'

'That will be great! You see, I don't have time to start over. To speed up the process and to deliver things on time, I'll have to use the resources of your serpentarium and Sudhir's skills in order to meet the deadline set by the Americans.'

'We'll definitely help you.'

'Why can't we get Sudhir on the phone right now?' he asked.

'Getting him on a phone call when he is up there, in Uttarakhand, is not possible. But I'll try my best to reach him.'

Though we needed money to break even and to pay the bank loan, the zeal that drove us to do things, and the passion that dragged us and made us stand on the brink of death every time we encountered venomous snakes had made us realize that doing things purely for the sake of money meant nothing. It was like dying before death or living just for the sake of living.

'Do you think this permutation and combination of environment, change in temperature and diet is really going to work?' I asked with a tinge of doubt in my mind.

'Oh, bilkul. It will definitely work,' Deepak said. His voice sounded informal and friendly for the first time and he continued his speech by giving examples that supported his theory. 'Two years ago, Singaporean scientists discovered a novel protein called haditoxin in king cobra venom. More research on haditoxin revealed that it could serve as a primary compound from which other drugs could be made to treat certain neurological conditions. So it is likely that haditoxin ... '

While he continued his yakity-yak on venom chemistry, my thoughts for some reason raced back in time and settled on Sudhir's mother's face, her wrinkle-free innocent face as I had seen it before she was reduced to ashes in an electric crematorium. She had died of a heart attack. When Deepak told me about molecules that could help cure cancer and heart disease, I was convinced that Sudhir would be more than happy to help, not for the sake of making money but for the sake of his parents.

Before I left his lab, Deepak said, 'I'll call you next week. Be ready! The main project stakeholders are monitoring the progress of VEN 40 from America. We need to show them something concrete before the end of this year. Call Sudhir and ask him to come soon. Goodbye!'

After hearing his parting words I was so overwhelmed that I forgot my way to exit the facility.

***

I went back to work, but I couldn't contact Sudhir over the phone. I wanted to brief him about VEN40. As promised, Deepak called me after one week. It was late, past seven in the evening, and he had told me to come to his place. The narrow road to Parel was crowded with traffic and all the vehicles were moving at a snail's pace. I told the taxi driver to drive faster as it was getting dark. Finally, I reached Deepak's place.

He made me sit on the couch and offered me masala tea. The refreshing taste settled my nerves and made me forget my tiring journey. We discussed VEN40 over dinner and Deepak told me to bring Sudhir to Haffkine Institute once he was back from Uttarakhand. After dinner, he briefed me on his plan and gave me a list of things he wanted from our Serpentarium.

I asked, 'Well, Deepak, any ideas on how Sudhir's participation in VEN40 will help you know more about king cobras?'

'As I told you, I'm not looking for snake catchers or venom milkers. I need someone who can get into the psyche of king cobras and understand them from the inside ... someone who knows what lurks inside their mind. I only deal with microscopes and molecules and don't know much about the behaviour of snakes. My mantra is very simple: if you want to get something new, you have to do something new. So to get something new out of king cobra venom, we have to put them in different environments, test them, and study their behaviour. And Sudhir knows a lot about king cobras, which will help me conduct some crazy experiments on them.'

Suddenly, I heard a faint beep coming from my shirt pocket and I realized that my mobile phone had run out of power.

'It's time for me to leave.'

Before leaving his house, Deepak said, 'We need results! There's a lot of work to be done and we're in a fight against time. If we end up finding something concrete, we might get a chance to present our findings in NYAS. I want to induct Sudhir into VEN40 as soon as possible.'

After saying goodbye I walked out of his house with pride and happiness swelling in me like an air balloon. Outside, the weather was sultry, the air smelled of traffic fumes, and I was on my way to Thane in a taxi.

***

I remember every detail of what had happened that night when I took a taxi to Thane, every single detail. And the problems that ensued when the taxi broke down near the highway. They changed my life completely and I still can't erase that night from my memory.

'Sir, you'll have to take another taxi,' said the taxi driver.

I got down from the taxi and decided to walk. Instead of taking the usual route, I decided to take a short-cut home. It was a moonless night and the sky was empty with no stars to fill the dark firmament. The road beside the lake leading to my place was deserted. Street lights that ran across the deserted road were poorly lit. A line of tall trees on both sides of the lane added to the poor visibility. Everything was bathed in a dull yellow. As I walked down the lane, I saw a dog curled up near an open dustbin. The dog woke up with a start and growled at me with its tail raised. The faint yellow street light cast a ghoulish glow in the dog's eyes. I shooed the dog away and it made a series of whimpering sounds before disappearing into the dark.

To my left stood a dilapidated building near the lake and next to the building was an abandoned temple. I walked past the building in a hurried manner and my heart thumped inside my chest. Though I had walked down this lane many times during busy morning hours, I felt a bit scared seeing the eeriness the same place offered at this time of night. I did all the things that one usually does while walking alone on an empty street; I looked behind to see if someone were stalking me, I wiped cold sweat from the back of my neck and nervously whistled my favourite song to feel better, but that didn't help.

Suddenly I heard a sharp cry. I looked back to find its source. After a few seconds of silence, I heard the plaintive cry again but this time it was low-pitched. To me, it seemed like a rumbling of a man in constant pain. I followed the sound and made my way closer to the abandoned temple near the building. When I reached the threshold of the temple, I saw a lit torch lying on the ground. Next to the torch was a dark figure lying motionless on the ground. *Hurry, run away from here,* my inner voice told me but inquisitiveness silenced it.

I took the torch and shone it on the black figure. I saw his boots first and then I saw blood.

I held my breath and ran the torch beam over him in an attempt to see his face. When I fixed the beam on his face, he mumbled something I didn't catch. His face was smeared with blood and his thick beard gave him a rugged look. His eyes popped out of his face. He was dying a slow death. *You will not touch him,* my inner voice said.

First he looked at me, and then he slowly turned his head sideways to fix his gaze on a revolver lying next to a pool of blood. Beads of saliva glistened on his lips. Blood spots dotted his white shirt. It took me a while to realize that I was standing in midst of a crime scene. I decided to run away but something lying on his chest caught my attention.

I leaned down for a closer look and saw several plastic packets filled with white chunky powder. I took one packet from the lot and sniffed it deeply. It smelled of some weird chemical. To me it definitely looked like a drug. With my limited knowledge of drugs I deduced the white crystalline powder was cocaine. When we were in college, Vinod and I confined ourselves to academics, but soon after we graduated Vinod wanted to try the "other-worldly experience" that his friends bragged about while taking drugs. As coke belongs to the rich and powerful, we travelled all the way to the richest urban precinct in India: South Mumbai – to snort it. We went to a posh hotel near Colaba Causeway and met a man who sold us half a gram of coke sealed in a small plastic bag. I sniffed the cover before making two thin lines, one for me and one for Vinod, and we snorted it like professionals but ended up coughing like amateurs. After the coughing incident we never tried coke again but the smell somehow got etched in my olfactory system.

After letting out a sigh of discomfort, the African turned expressionless. I couldn't figure out whether he had some life left in him. But I could see his fingers moving. *It's time to leave!* My inner voice warned me. It took me some time to realize that I had accidentally walked into the aftermath of a drug deal gone askew. A soft breeze cooled me and my sweat. I felt better. And in that moment of clarity I decided to leave without a second thought.

As I turned to make my way home I heard footsteps. Sensing danger, I dropped the torch and took a few quick steps to find a hiding place. Minutes later I was standing behind the temple wall. The footsteps grew louder and came closer. I craned my head to see something. Then I saw a shadow. It was the shadow of a man with a gun in his hand. I craned over to the right to get a clear view. In the glare from the dim street light, I could see a man walking towards the dead man. He stopped near him, put his gun in the back of his pants, and did the same thing that I had done. After sniffing one packet from the lot he signalled to somebody. Another man appeared with a gun in his hand and to me he looked like a cop. I began to feel sick and blew out my breath impatiently. Then I heard one of the policeman cough. They said something. I strained my ears to hear them but I couldn't make out anything. I looked for options to escape. And when I decided to slither away soundlessly, I felt something hard on the back of my head.

'Hands up, don't try to do anything stupid.' said a deep voice behind me.

I turned slowly and saw a dark brown face. It was a 40-something man with a tired look on his face. He stared at me, his eyes scanned my features, analyzing and registering my appearance in that dim light. I stared back at him with rage but I knew I was no match for him as he was armed with a gun and looked like a cop. Holding a loaded gun pointed at my chest, he looked at me with arrogance and behaved as if I was one of the most notorious drug lords of all time. In a desperate attempt to prove my innocence I smiled nervously, avoiding direct eye contact and spoke sympathetically.

'You've got the wrong guy! I was just walking ... on my way... home ... then I heard some noise ...' I stuttered badly and I couldn't complete my sentence.

He ignored my plea and signalled to the other two officers to join him.

'Do you hear me? You've got the wrong guy! I saw him lying motionless and I panicked.'

He grinned and punched me in my face. I tripped and fell on my back. Before I could say another word he kicked and stomped me viciously. My face turned red and my body was dotted with painful bruises.

'Is he your partner?' he asked.

'No! I told you ... I was just walking and I heard some noise ...'

He kicked me again. And even in that gripping pain I continued my speech in a calm, firm voice.

'I heard some noise ... and I saw this man ... lying here ... There was ... There was blood everywhere ...'

'Is he alive?' he asked one of the police officers.

'No heartbeat, sir.'

'You fuckin' mule,' he exploded. 'You killed him.'

I murmured as pain overtook me, my thoughts and my words. Grabbing my collar in one hand, he lifted me to my feet and pinned me against the temple wall. The dim light of the streetlamp caught his eye and made him look devilish.

'Tell me about the drug deal, you fuckin' mule!' he exclaimed.

'I – I don't know what you're talking about.'

'I am talking about the fuckin' drug deal you fuckin' mule.'

He clenched his teeth while saying it. Initially, I was wondering why he was calling me the offspring of a male donkey and a female horse, but it dawned on me that I was being referred to as a drug mule who smuggles illegal drugs.

'I – I really don't know what you're talking about.'

He stared at me gallingly and then called someone over the walkie-talkie. Within five minutes, a police jeep with flashing lights had stopped beside me. Three uniformed cops got out and surrounded me, forming a semicircle.

'You've got the wrong guy! Please believe me,' I pleaded in a submissive voice.

'Get in,' the officer grumbled. I stepped into the back of the jeep. Twenty minutes later, the jeep entered the police compound and screeched to a halt. The cops got down and dragged me to the police station, poking and hitting me mercilessly.

'Check his pockets,' said the senior police officer.

They tied my hands behind my back and checked me thoroughly. And at that very moment I realized that my phone was missing. It was early morning when they locked me in the jail cell. I was exhausted. And I couldn't say a word.

'Give him some water. I'll see him in the afternoon,' said the senior police officer.

***

Will someone help me? Should I contact Sudhir? If I contact him will he get in trouble? These thoughts crowded my mind and made me weary. *Will I ever get out of this hell hole?* I asked myself. I slept for a while and woke up with a start on hearing the clinking sound of metal on metal. The guards brought me out of my cell and made me sit in a chair. I saw the senior police officer standing with a lathi in his hand, swirling it playfully.

'Did he say anything?' he asked one of his subordinates.

'No, sir.'

'I'll get the truth out of him. Do you have a family? Kids?' he asked me.

'No.'

'Father?'

'He's no more; he died in a tragic accident.'

'Mother?'

'She died too.'

'So you are a loner?'

'Yes.'

'So, what the deal was about?'

I kept mum.

'Tell me more about the gang? What's the deal with you and that dead guy?' he asked.

'I don't know anything!'

After each question he kicked me in the groin, expecting a satisfactory answer, which would crack the cocaine case and help him track down the actual source of the drug. My innocent answers agitated him.

'Your tricks won't work against me,' he said, grinding his teeth. Then he grabbed my collar and pulled me close enough that I could see the small brass nameplate on his chest. It read: Murali Rao – Assistant Commissioner of Police.

The minute hand on the clock moved like a snail as Murali grilled me with questions on the cocaine packets. Everyone assumed that I was the mastermind behind this so-called drug deal. I wanted to convey the message to the outside world that I was trapped inside this hellhole. *Who can help me?* I asked myself. Definitely not Sudhir – he could be dragged too – they could even label him as my partner in crime. After much deliberation, I decided to contact Vinod; being a research scientist with good links, he was my last hope.

***

From the local police station they transferred me to Arthur Road Jail. It was hard for me to believe that I was sent to jail with no evidence of my involvement in the crime but being at the wrong place made my case weak. I was put in a cell which begged for space and sanitation. It was Murali's idea to send me to Arthur Road Jail so as to test my endurance. The cops did not believe my serpentarium story and they traced Sudhir through me. After some groundwork they figured out that Sudhir was in Uttarakhand when this incident took place. So they took him off of their suspect list and held me solely responsible for everything that had happened on that fateful night. I was lodged in a high-security cell crammed with drug dealers, rapists and other hardened criminals. Life was tough. I was in Arthur for a week or two. To tell you the truth, I lost all sense of time in that tiny torture cell. Then, I was shifted to the more spacious Taloja Central jail in Navi Mumbai.

I owe my life to Vinod as he engineered my escape from Taloja. Soon after my escape, I called him from a public phone booth and thanked him. Next on my list was Sudhir. I heaved a sigh of relief when I heard his voice. He was travelling and his inquisitive *hello* was interspersed with the constant rhythm of a moving train.

'I've been calling you for days and your phone was switched off all the time!' complained Sudhir.

'I lost my phone. Where are you now?'

'I'm on my way to Mumbai. I'll reach in an hour or two.'

I harrumphed and said "okay."

'You sound worried and tensed. Are you alright? Is everything okay?' he asked.

'I need to discuss something important, but I can't discuss it over the phone. After you get to Mumbai, come to Khopoli,' I said in a hush-hush voice.

'Where in Khopoli?'

'Our usual place,' I said and disconnected the call.

***

Our meeting place in Khopoli was a warehouse owned by a friend I had met while building the Serpentarium. Far from Khopoli station, amidst small factories, this old warehouse was the safest place for a secret rendezvous. After gaining access to the warehouse with the help of my friend, I waited for Sudhir to arrive. It was stuffy inside. Sweat trickled down my back like a free-flowing rivulet. Gazing at the closed shutter, I felt claustrophobic. Moments later, there was a violent pounding on the shutter. I ran over to open it. My heart thwacked my rib cage as I lifted it up halfway and stopped. I leaned down to get a better view. It was Sudhir, standing with a cautious look on his face. Within seconds, I dragged him inside the warehouse and closed the shutter. He looked startled for a moment, and then composed himself upon seeing my face.

'You scared the hell out of me,' he said.

'Shh! don't shout!' I pleaded.

'Why are you being so guarded and secretive?

'I have some good news and some bad news for you. Tell me which one you want to hear first,' I said and smiled wryly.

Sudhir wanted to hear the bad news first. With a heavy heart, I told him about the repercussions of being in the wrong place at the wrong time and the series of unfortunate events that had followed after my taxi broke down.

'That's so fucking unfortunate,' he said. 'Who got you out?'

'My friend Vinod,' I said. 'Though you do not know him, I've told him about you.'

'Sorry I couldn't help you!' he said. 'I had to extend my stay to teach Advanced Mountaineering to a fresh batch of students. I tried calling you but you were not reachable.'

'That's okay,' I said. 'Your interference in this issue would have complicated the matter. These guys could have pulled you over and got you involved in the case.'

I saw a gleam of amusement in Sudhir's face when I told him about the VEN40 project and my meeting with Deepak Malekar.

'They are expecting concrete results by end of this year. You'll have to fulfil our dreams,' I said.

'I'll try my best! What's our next move?' asked Sudhir.

A series of next moves popped up like bubbles and crowded my grey cells. It had come all at once that I had to catalogue it to give it some structure.

First move: To avoid being in public places and to mask myself by wearing a burqa so as to escape the police.

Second move: To introduce Sudhir to Deepak and make Sudhir an important member of the VEN40 project.

Third move: To clear the bank loan by accepting Deepak's deal.

'Let's meet Deepak as soon as possible,' said Sudhir.

***

Deepak sat down in an armchair with a surprised look on his face. Seeing me wearing a burqa made him smirk but when I briefed him on the string of unfortunate events that followed after I left his place that night, he sympathised with me instantly.

'Holy shit! That's unfortunate! You know, you really had me worried. I tried calling you but you were not reachable,' said Deepak.

Though he asked us a few questions about the incident, his mind did not dwell on it for long. 'Okay, let's get started! We have a deadline to meet,' he said.

Without wasting much time, I introduced Sudhir to Deepak.

'I've heard a lot about you,' said Deepak and shot him a warm smile.

After a friendly handshake, Deepak asked him about his academic qualifications and Sudhir's reply startled him.

'I am a college drop-out.'

'But he has intuitive knowledge of venom and snakes,' I said, backing him up.

Minutes after the introductory session, what followed was an hour-long conversation about venom and venom chemistry, and I stood there, gaping at them like an interloper. It took no time for Deepak to realize that he was conversing with a genius who was also a self-taught herpetologist. Apart from being an expert snake handler, Sudhir was good at chromatography – a biochemical process of separating proteins and enzymes from snake venom. After exhausting the topics related to snake venom, Deepak emphasized the importance of the project and discussed the pharmaceutical industry in general.

'Today, new drug development in the pharmaceutical industry is on the decline. Strict drug safety regulations and non-conducive climate for clinical trials are stumbling blocks on the path to developing innovative drugs. VEN40 aims to study the special chemical makeup of cobra venom. Our objective is to overcome these stumbling blocks and create innovative drugs that are commercially viable.'

'I'd like to visit your facility in Haffkine,' said Sudhir.

Everything went according to our plan. Deepak was happy to induct Sudhir into the exclusive VEN40 team. I had no choice but to opt out of the project. With a heavy heart I wished him luck and hugged Sudhir tightly. It was an emotional farewell as tears rolled from my eyes like small streams.

'What will you do?' asked Sudhir. 'Where will you hide?'

'Don't worry! I'll find some place.'

'What if the police come to our Serpentarium, asking about your whereabouts?'

'Tell them you haven't seen me for the past two months.'

'What if they arrest Sudhir?' asked Deepak.

'No, they cannot arrest Sudhir without any evidence. If they do it, it will be illegal. I got caught because I was there, right there. But Sudhir is nowhere in the picture as he was in Uttarakhand at the time. Without solid evidence everyone is just a suspect. They caught me red-handed – that's what they think, but I could have played a waiting game to prove my innocence as they had no solid proof to convict me. They put me in Arthur to get something out of me, to get solid proof. They wanted some evidence to pronounce me guilty. Escaping from prison was not a good idea as it strengthened their wrong opinion of me but I had to escape to fulfil our dreams and turn them into reality. I had no choice,' I said.

Before leaving Deepak's place, I hugged Sudhir tight and wished him good luck. That was the last time I saw him. After that, I spoke to him twice over the phone. I called him after he met Deepak in his lab at Haffkine Institute. He told me of his role in exploring the therapeutic effects of king cobra venom. And on the day he boarded the flight for New York, I phoned him and said, 'All the best! We did it!'

I think it is time for me to stop as the sun is peering at me through the gap in the mountains. I'll have to find another hiding place. Oh! I'll have to run now! Yes, I think it is time for me to stop.

***

The day that Deepak was waiting for finally arrived. He took off his glasses and gazed at Sudhir in silent wonderment. The true meaning of Eureka was seen in his face and he was ecstatic. Sudhir watched as he began to show his white teeth, and then he raised his hands in victory. He looked as if he knew the answers to all of life's questions. His eyes were gleaming with delight.

'Did you find anything interesting?' asked Sudhir.

'Last night, I was working with a tiny fraction of Indian king cobra venom, and while studying its structure I was able to identify a new protein. I found it to be nontoxic up to 8mg/kg, so I tested it on lab mice to see its effect. And I got some interesting results.'

'What did you see?'

'I observed certain neurological effects.'

'That's great news!' said Sudhir and punched his fist in the air.

'There's still a lot of work to be done,' said Deepak, subduing his enthusiasm. 'We'll have to find ways to isolate specific parts of this new protein in order to detoxify it and manipulate it to our advantage.'

'We'll have to give this novel protein some name if we happen to present it in a research paper,' said Sudhir.

'I haven't thought of a name. It is a small protein made up of 108 amino acids. And it has an unusual makeup when compared to other king cobra venoms. I was not able to get anything out of Malaysian, Indonesian or Chinese king cobras. This protein definitely has some affinity with the Indian species,' said Deepak.

'In that case, I'll get more Indian cobras and milk them for you,' said Sudhir.

Deepak asked about the snake whose venom had the right cocktail to create an impact in the neurological system of mice. At Deepak's request, Sudhir traced the venom to its actual source and showed him a 14-foot female Indian king cobra.

'I got her last month,' said Sudhir. 'To start with, I gave her some Flagyl to make her feel better and kept her in a separate glass enclosure. She weighed 5.60 kg on the day of arrival.'

'Did you feed her a special diet?' asked Deepak.

'She didn't eat anything for the first two days. Many kings refuse to eat in captivity. On the third day, I offered her two large pieces of corn snake and she ate them in a jiffy. Then I offered her rodents, lizards, other snakes and gallons of fresh water, nothing special,' said Sudhir.

'Get more venom out of her,' said Deepak.

'She takes two weeks to give out fresh venom, so we'll have to wait for at least a week. I can get some new Indian kings for you if you want,' said Sudhir.

'I've been dealing with Indian kings all my life. This one is special, really special!' said Deepak. 'Where did you get her?'

'I found her in a forest near Shahapur. When I saw her, she was building a nest for her eggs. Twisting and turning herself, she was slowly gathering dry leaves and other debris to construct a nest. I tracked her for a week as she stood guard over her nest like a king guarding his territory. Being a pregnant mom, she was aggressive. Her eyes spoke of fear and vengeance when she saw me nearing her nest. It took me almost an hour to catch her. I think she's special because she's pregnant,' said Sudhir.

'In that case, get me some expecting mothers,' said Deepak.

'It's not that easy. They don't mate whenever they want, like humans. For them mating is not a pleasure but an instinct put in by nature to reproduce and the act is driven by the seasons. Kings mate once a year. It's very difficult to find expecting mothers,' said Sudhir.

'Indian kings reach sexual maturity at six years of age. During the month of January, male king cobras go looking for sex and female king cobras give off a special scent that attracts males of their kind. But sometimes, finding a female is not easy as I have seen males wandering, spending weeks or months trying to find a female. Being cannibalistic, they sometimes eat their own kind and that makes their courtship a difficult business as the male king cobra could eat a female, thereby putting an end to their mating. So, one has to be lucky to spot a pregnant female king cobra.'

'Can they be successfully bred in captivity? Any known instances?' asked Deepak.

'Yes, they can be successfully bred in captivity and I have my own breeding centre near Thane.'

'But I've read that king cobras rarely breed in captivity and so far only two cases have been recorded. Is that true?' questioned Deepak.

'That's hogwash! The literature about king cobras is full of guesswork. Two years ago, I visited Shivaram Karanth Biological Park near Mangalore to see baby king cobras that had been born and raised in captivity. Four out of five pairs mated in captivity and three females went on to lay 147 eggs in all. They had the right infrastructure in place to make it happen,' said Sudhir.

'Why don't we do this in our facility?' asked Deepak.

'It's not possible as kings won't mate in cramped glass enclosures. They are too shy to do that. And undertaking captive breeding is a cumbersome job. Though it is difficult to make them mate in captivity, it is doable if you simulate natural forest conditions in the enclosure. For that you need a lot of space. And you need a lot of money. I found success by creating an off-display enclosure mimicking the Western Ghats. I monitored their movements closely through closed-circuit TVs. I tasted success when three out of five pairs mated in my snake park and two females went on to lay 68 eggs in total,' said Sudhir.

'When did this happen?'

'Recently,' said Sudhir.

'So, you have two young mothers in your Serpentarium.'

'Yes, but they are not from the forest and the one you are dealing with comes from the forest. My guess is that the venom composition of a home-grown cobra is different and you may not find your wonder protein in their venom.'

'I'll figure that out,' said Deepak. 'Just get them for me.'

'Sure,' said Sudhir. 'You can even use them for your future experiments as females have the ability to store sperm for several years and produce baby cobras up to three years after their last contact with a male snake.'

'That's amazing! Bring them to me! Let's get this started!'

***

Sudhir gave Deepak his home-grown young mothers. He milked venom from them and Deepak was able to find his wonder protein in all the samples. Deepak repeated his experiment with other young mother snakes from Indonesia, China and Malaysia, and got the same results.

'For some reason, female kings seem to produce this protein soon after laying eggs or after getting pregnant,' said Deepak.

'That's true! So what's the next step?' asked Sudhir.

'We'll report our findings to the New York Academy of Sciences. I'm sure they will be impressed by our results. This protein can be manipulated to treat diseases of the nervous system. Even cancers that affect the nervous system can be cured.'

'What about clinical trials?'

'It's a tough road ahead but I'm sure we'll make it through the phases of clinical trials.'

'Is it a potential drug candidate?' asked Sudhir. His question was definitely valid as many molecular discoveries at the laboratory die a quick death and never make it to the drug store.

'Yes, I'm confident!' replied Deepak. He continued his experiments and tasted success. Of the experiments he had performed in his lab, two were significant. The first one was about delivering pain relief through his wonder protein and the second finding startled the entire VEN40 team. His wonder protein was able to nurse damaged motor neurons.

***

ALS – Amyotrophic lateral sclerosis, also known as Charcot disease, is a fatal neurodegenerative disease which was first described by Jean-Martin Charcot – a famous French neurologist. Though ALS is incurable, it remained largely unknown to the general public until it affected a famous baseball player by the name of Lou Gehrig in 1939. The world also learned about it when it affected the famous theoretical physicist Stephen Hawking in 1963, confining him to a wheelchair. A look at the statistics shows that ALS is responsible for nearly two deaths per hundred thousand people annually. Despite the fact that ALS occurs throughout the world with no racial, ethnic or socioeconomic boundaries, it seems to have an affinity for Americans. It is estimated that as many as 30,000 Americans may have the disease at any given time and about 5600 people in the US are diagnosed with ALS each year. It is estimated that by 2050, nearly 15 million Americans will have ALS and other neurological disorders.

One hundred and fifty years of research have been futile as the medical world is yet to find a cure for ALS. Though researchers have come up with several attractive theories on the possible causes of ALS, the exact cause is still not known. So far, scientists have only managed to find a life extension for patients in the form of Riluzole, a drug approved by the FDA in 1995. It slows the progress of ALS, but no medicine seems able to halt or reverse the condition.

Apart from Riluzole, the use of non-invasive ventilation, breathing through a mask that fits over the mouth and nose, was shown to prolong survival between eight and eleven months. ALS is a careless killer and the life expectancy of an ALS patient averages between two to five years from the time of diagnosis. Some patients live longer, but the crippling disease finally kills its victims – slowly and steadily.

'This wonder protein will definitely cure ALS and might even reverse the effects,' said Deepak confidently. He was addressing a small gathering of the team at Haffkine Institute.

'ALS has got nothing to do with muscles. Muscle weakness in just an effect and not the actual cause. When the disease hits you, it affects large nerve cells that exist in the brain and spinal cord. Ideally, in healthy grey matter, messages from the upper motor neurons in the brain are transmitted to the lower motor neurons in the spinal cord, and from them to particular muscles. In the case of ALS, both the upper and lower motor neurons die, and eventually the muscles die but these degenerating nerve cells can be nursed back to health by placing our wonder protein in the affected areas. By injecting it into the spinal cord of patients with ALS, we hope to stop the degeneration of nerve cells. This even has the potential to reverse the effects by making the nerve cells healthy. Also, the benefits of our protein can be extended beyond ALS as it falls under the MND label.

'The terms Motor Neuron Disease and ALS are sometimes used interchangeably. However, MND is an umbrella term for different types of neurological disorders with ALS being just one of them. Many diseases fall under MND : ALS, Primary lateral sclerosis (PLS), Hereditary spastic paraparesis (HSP), Progressive bulbar palsy (PBP), Spinal muscular atrophy (SMA), Kennedy disease and Post polio syndrome (PPS). I'm confident that our wonder drug has the right proteins to cure all types of MND. We hope to get it FDA-approved as soon as possible and break the rigid monopoly that Rilutek has built. Moreover, Rilutek is not an ideal drug; some ALS specialists do not recommend it. Though it provides a life extension of three months, it does not stop ALS in its tracks. Another aspect is affordability – my drug will be low-priced in the market!'

After hearing his speech, Sudhir clapped first and slowly other team members joined him, making it a thunderous applause. The upcoming event organized by the NYAS in association with the ALS Society of Canada would be Deepak's ticket to opulence and glory. It was plain that this event, frequented by academic researchers, industry scientists and government representatives, was his golden chance to have an impact. Before leaving Haffkine, Deepak told Sudhir about the travel plan.

'We'll be flying to New York to present our findings.'

***

Sudhir sat next to the taxi driver and stared out the window to catch a glimpse of Mumbai in a festive mood. Trees were decorated with colour-changing LED lights. Besides the fireworks, restaurants and bars were playing loud music to lure the masses with their New Year's Eve parties. 'Go fast!' Sudhir said to the taxi driver. The driver nodded politely and honked. Because it was New Year's Eve, traffic was heavy on the road to the airport. Deepak, who had reached the airport before him, called Sudhir to find out about his whereabouts. 'I'm stuck in traffic. You proceed, I'll join you,' said Sudhir and told the driver to hurry up or take an alternate short route. After a wait of about thirty minutes, the traffic cleared and Sudhir reached just in time.

***

It was supposed to be a bit dark outside the airport, but the tall, new air traffic control tower stood like a blazing torch illuminating the scene. Numerous head- and tail-lights injected liveliness into the nightlife of the city. A network of street lights spread across the length and breadth of Mumbai brightened it, adding to the oft-repeated phrase: Mumbai never sleeps.

There was a sense of excitement in the air as the world was bidding farewell to the old year and gearing up to welcome the new. The year 2016 was just a few hours away and around half of Mumbai's population was welcoming it by dancing and singing under electrifying disco lights in a drunken haze. Migrants desperate to get to their hometowns were clogging the departure points: the airport, railway stations, bus stops and taxi stands. Outside the airport, dazzling fireworks decorated the dark sky with stunning colours. And inside the airport, the overall mood was upbeat.

Chhatrapati Shivaji International Airport was crowded and one could hear the constant chatter of people, the ringing of cell phones and the boarding announcements alerting passengers of the departure of their flights. High-quality duty-free merchandise in charming boutiques lured foreigners by offering great discounts. Many travellers were whiling away their time by catching up with friends on Twitter or Facebook on their laptop computers using free Wi-Fi hotspots. Mobile phones were beeping and vibrating with New Year messages. News footage was running on televisions. One screen showed a genetically edited baby saying, *I want a mobile phone and I want a laptop. I don't want reality! I want virtual reality!* Another screen featured a scientist posing a question, *Is Science and Technology making this world more predictable? Or is it the other way around? Has science brought order out of chaos? Or chaos out of order?*

Abhishek Patil straightened his tie in the colours of the Indian flag and tied his shoestrings. He walked through the security check-in with a smile on his face and adjusted his overcoat before speaking briefly to one of the air hostesses accompanying him. 'I am going to complete 20,000 flying hours soon,' he remarked. His voice brimmed with arrogance and pride.

Ten minutes later, a high-pitched voice emerged from the flight announcement system. *This is the pre-boarding announcement for flight AI 605 to New York. We are now inviting those passengers with small children, and any passengers requiring special assistance, to begin boarding at this time. Please have your boarding pass and identification ready. Regular boarding will begin in approximately twenty minutes' time. Thank you.*

Boeing 777-300, the metallic marvel, was standing at the gate. Patil spoke to the flight attendant about the weather conditions and ride reports. 'Everything is okay sir, we are good to go,' she said. 'Tell Rakesh to do the walk-around,' said Patil and went to grab a cup of coffee from the terminal before setting up his side of the cockpit.

Rakesh Mehra was the first officer on flight AI 605 and had been Patil's second-in-command for almost two years. He was the flying pilot, though Captain Patil was responsible for the aircraft, its passengers, and the crew. Being a long-haul flight, Jatin Doshi had been added to the crew as a relief pilot to assist Rakesh during his rest periods.

As instructed by the captain, Rakesh took a stroll and inspected the overall condition of the aircraft, checking the tire pressure, the status of the oxygen bottles in the cockpit, the wear on the brakes, the engine fan blades for any nicks, and finally eyed the entire airplane for fuel, oil or hydraulic leaks.

Sudhir was hurrying through the proceedings to get his boarding pass while Deepak waited for him at Gate 3. He sat for a while to catch his breath and suddenly, a hasty voice emerged from the flight announcement system. *This is the final boarding call for passengers Sudhir Shivaram, Murali Rao, Vandana Rao, Vinod Johri and Ram Johal booked on flight AI 605 to New York. Please proceed to gate no. 3 immediately. The final checks are being completed and the captain will order for the doors of the aircraft to close in approximately ten minutes time. I repeat. This is the final boarding call for Sudhir Shivaram, Murali Rao, Vandana Rao, Vinod Johri and Ram Johal booked on flight AI 605 to New York. Thank you.*

After hearing the announcement Sudhir got up with a start and walked towards the gate.

Meanwhile, in the cockpit, Patil and Rakesh tested their oxygen masks and inspected all the electrical circuit breakers to make sure they were in place. Engine fire detection systems were tested resulting in a bell sound that one might usually hear while boarding the airplane. Rakesh checked everything meticulously: Auxiliary fuel pump – Off, Flight controls – Free and correct, Instruments and Radios – checked and set, Landing gear position lights – Checked, Altimeter – Set, Directional gyro – Set, Fuel gauges – Checked, Trim – Set, Propeller – Exercise, Magnetos – Checked, Engine idle – Checked, Flaps – As required, Seat belts / shoulder harnesses – Fastened, Parking brake – Off, Doors and windows – Locked.

'Sir, we are good to go,' he said to Captain Patil and recited a lengthy, boring pre-flight announcement like a school kid who'd been told to recite multiplication tables. *Ladies and gentleman, welcome onboard Flight AI 605 with non- stop service from Mumbai to New York. We are currently fourth in line for take-off and are expected to be in the air in approximately ten minutes' time. We ask that you fasten your seatbelts at this time and secure all baggage underneath your seat or in the overhead compartments. We also ask that your seats and table trays remain in the upright position for take-off. Please turn off all personal electronic devices, including laptops and cell phones or set your electronic devices to airplane mode until an announcement is made upon arrival. Smoking is not allowed on board, including in the lavatories. Also, use of electronic cigarettes is not allowed. Tampering with, disabling or destroying the smoke detectors in the lavatories is prohibited by law.*

One of the air hostesses signalled to the other flight attendants to stand in their respective places, equidistant from each other, and when they were ready to enact her words into actions, she addressed the passengers on safety measures, her voice soft and sweet like a fine wine.

Ladies and gentlemen, on behalf of the crew I ask that you please direct your attention to the monitors above as we review the emergency procedures. There are six emergency exits on this aircraft. Take a minute to locate the exit closest to you. Note that the nearest exit may be behind you. Count the number of rows to this exit.

In the plane, Deepak was sitting right behind Sudhir. He rummaged through his bag to find a copy of his research paper without paying any heed to the emergency procedures that were being recited.

In the event of an emergency, please assume the bracing position. Lean forward with your hands on top of your head and your elbows against your thighs. Ensure your feet are flat on the floor. Should the cabin experience sudden pressure loss, stay calm and listen for instructions from the cabin crew. Oxygen masks will drop down from above your seat. Place the mask over your mouth and nose, like this.

Sudhir chuckled at the sight of the air hostess keeping the oxygen mask over her mouth and nose, for he had survived at high altitudes all his life. Having dealt with venomous snakes throughout his life, he was an expert in dealing with danger.

Pull the strap to tighten it. If you are travelling with children, make sure that your own mask is on first before helping your children. In the unlikely event of an emergency landing and evacuation, leave your carry-on items behind. A life vest is located in a pouch under your seat or between the armrests.

Sudhir closed his eyes for a moment and remembered Peter.

While we wait for take-off, please take a moment to review the safety data in the seat pocket in front of you.

The runway was cleared for take-off. Captain Abhishek Patil spoke into the microphone *Flight attendants prepare for take-off please.*

The engine started buzzing; the aircraft began its accelerating run along the runway, and within a few minutes, AI 605 was just a tiny speck in the sky, a blip on the radar. Cruising at an altitude of 20,000 feet, at airspeed of 300 miles per hour, AI 605 was flying above the clouds where the air started to thin and it was also getting smoother. Just then, a voice came cutting through the cabin air trying to get some attention of the passengers on board.

Ladies and gentlemen, the Captain has turned off the Fasten Seat Belt sign, and you may now move around the cabin. However, we always recommend keeping your seat belt fastened while you're seated. You may now turn on your electronic devices such as cell phones, and laptops, but we suggest keeping them on airplane mode.

Deepak sat engrossed reviewing his research paper while Sudhir couldn't think of anything but Peter.

In a few moments, the flight attendants will be passing around the cabin to offer you hot or cold drinks, as well as a light snack and you can use the monitor in front of you to browse our in-flight entertainment. Now, sit back, relax, and enjoy the flight. Thank you.

The relief pilot, Jatin Doshi, sat near the controls, watching all the glowing buttons and levers in the cockpit. After six hours of smooth flying, fast rivers of air outside shook the plane, causing turbulence strong enough to judder a glass of orange juice kept on the tray table.

***

Story 3

Chapter 3: Silent Malady

Some months before the present day

Minutes after the clouds took on the colour of soot, the rains followed. Big, round, silvery drops fell mercilessly against the window panes, like an unwanted guest trying to enter the house through the window. Rains made the narrow, dirty roads of Kurla dirtier.

Murali, sitting on the balcony, was reading a news article about himself. *Senior Inspector Murali Rao was appointed the new Assistant Commissioner of Police, Anti-Narcotics Cell, Mumbai. After taking charge as the city's Police Commissioner, Mr Rao told reporters, "It's really a dream come true for a young lad from Kurla slums to become Mumbai's Commissioner of Police."*

In the kitchen, his wife was making *kheer* and other delicacies to celebrate his promotion. Tempted by the smell of *kheer* he spoke to her in a demanding tone of voice. 'Where is my *kheer*? I am getting late for work.'

'Have patience, ACP, have patience,' she said teasingly.

The local newspapers boasted about his recent achievements. He read on.

Acting on a tip-off, Murali Rao and his team busted an inter-state gang of drug peddlers trying to smuggle 34kg of cannabis into the city. All were arrested on the spot.

A week ago, Murali and his team arrested four drug peddlers and seized around 2kg of heroin worth lakhs of rupees.

In another case, Murali Rao and his team laid a trap near Mulund, in which three drug peddlers were arrested. They were found in possession of 100 grams of Amphetamine worth 9 lakhs.

Even his dog, Tiger, stood proudly at his side and threatened every passer-by with a constant low-pitched growl. After getting his dose of information from the newspaper, Murali folded it into a rectangle and walked into the living room.

'Is there something to eat apart from *kheer*?' he asked, sitting at the dining table. Tiger sat at his side.

'First have hot, hot *kheer*,' his wife said, and poured the thick white liquid into a steel tumbler.

'Here, take it,' she offered.

What happened next was something odd, something unusual. The tumbler slipped from his hand and the *kheer* splashed everywhere, leaving a white stain on his uniform and on the black table cloth.

'You should have been careful while holding it,' his wife said.

Murali cursed his wife and told her that it was her mistake. The white stain was just the beginning and as time went by, things took a turn for the worse.

***

'Every man is born different, but culture and society cripple his uniqueness and suck him into the abyss of mediocrity. You are nothing but an extension of your religion, society and traditions! That's why everyone wants to be free. Go outside, and you'll see sad, gloomy faces everywhere; they all seek freedom. Freedom from monotony! Freedom from boredom! Freedom from the general problems of life! And that's when we chip in and give them what they want: absolute freedom from all earthly troubles! Enlightenment! Happiness! Bliss!

'Speaking about drugs and sex is taboo in this country and those who ban drugs actually end up creating a demand for them. Prohibition of drugs is not helpful to humanity; on the contrary, it becomes an invitation. When you say no to something, you actually make it more appealing. That's human psychology. And the day government officials and police realize this simple psychological fact, we'll be out of business.

'Punishing drug traffickers and addicts by imprisoning them makes no sense to me. In fact, jail is a place where drugs are freely available. By bribing the cops, addicts snort cocaine right here. Getting drugs into prison is a big business. A buddy of mine smuggles drugs into jail, through the guards, and the inmates pay a high price without a second thought.

'Let's talk about our business. We deal with cocaine and, like Hindu gods, it has many names, but in our gang we call it Charlie or Coke. When you are out there on the streets, talking to customers, you don't use the real name and if you do, you'll be fucked. Being an amateur you should be careful while selling coke.

'Virtually all cocaine, even the kind that you see on my table, comes from three countries: Bolivia, Colombia and Peru. The international drug mafia smuggles it into India from South

America via Hong Kong. Raw coca leaves when chewed or consumed as tea is good for health, but the human mind wants pleasure, pure pleasure! So we chop the coca leaves and mix it with chemicals and gas and sometimes even add acid. Finally, what you get is a white paste and when you put it to dry in the sun, it turns into a white chunky powder. When you make lines and snort this shit, you're transported to a new world. You'll experience euphoria! And within seconds, you'll forget what gravity is.

'Cocaine attracts the rich and the young. We cater to high-society groups in Mumbai, including entrepreneurs, businessmen, lawyers, industrialists, politicians, fashion designers and Bollywood stars. Some people snort coke just to flaunt!

'There are two types of cocaine users: recreational ones, and addicts. Your job is to deal with the first type. You'll have to look out for young, moneyed junkies between the ages of 19 and 32. They use cocaine at rave parties and spend an average of Rs 50,000 per week. Once you graduate with flying colours, you'll get to deal with addicts. They are our cash cows. If they don't consume one gram a day, they'll go berserk! They'll hand over their life on a platter to snort coke. And the funny part is that addicts never accept that they are addicts. To experience a quick high, addicts mix cocaine with water and inject the solution into the body. Sometimes, to get an instant hit, they use a freebase form of cocaine that can be smoked by heating the rocks with a candle or a lighter. When the vapour hits the brain, the devil is invited!

'As a novice, your target is to sell five grams every month, along with coke accessories like a glass vial, spoon, nasal sniffer, syringe and candles! Do you think you can manage it? You have to … or else you'll be sacked. Just like corporates, we have sales targets and review meetings. Business is business!

To maximize your returns, you'll have to find guys addicted to multiple drugs.

'A word of warning: don't sniff coke or you'll die quickly. Always remember, we're businessmen and our job is to provide what the customer wants. Don't even try to sample their *maal*; you'll get kicked in the brain. Just one sniff and you'll be on all fours, crawling like a baby! Anyhow, you look too naïve to be a junkie!

'Pure cocaine is difficult to get these days. When we get it, it's only 80% coke and, mind you, cocaine is damn expensive! So, we cut it with chemicals to make more money. While selling coke, the weight of the *maal* matters, not the contents. So, we cut it further and make it 50% drug and 50% something shitty! You can cut it with baking powder or lactose which looks like cocaine, but then customer will think the *maal* is weak and never buy from us again. The trick is to add something cheap that will mimic the effects of cocaine. I cut it with pain relievers like benzocaine which numbs the nose and mouth in the same way as cocaine does, so junkies think the *maal* is pure and original. You may slap me by saying that's being unethical in an unethical business, but that's how we book profits.

'Apart from selling *maal* your job is to buy cutting agents from the dealers. I'll teach you cutting techniques and how to fool customers into thinking they are snorting original *maal*. Some junkies die when they snort adulterated *maal* but who cares? They are going to lose themselves and die anyway. And sometimes we make it so shitty that even cops can't figure out the ingredients in our customers' blood. But we'll have to handle things in such a way that our reputation is not damaged.

'Well, I forgot to introduce myself; I'm the notorious Dawood Ibrahim!

'That was a joke, buddy.

'Listen. You need a lot of courage to do this job. You have to sell shit and put the money in my pocket. In a way, it is a noble job as you'll be feeding all the drug addicts who are hungry and waiting and loafing around to get a high. To start with, you'll need a good mentor. Ram Johal will teach you all the tricks of the trade. The lessons that you'll learn from him are invaluable, so learn them well and, who knows, you could be the next drug kingpin!' said Ali and looked up at Ram with a wicked smile.

***

It was night when Inspector More returned to the HQ of the Anti-Narcotics Cell (ANC) on Cuffe Parade. Murali was sitting in his chair, sporting his new ACP uniform. A bright light above his head gave the little stars on his badge a silvery sheen. His deep, broad chest stretched his uniform on both sides to reveal the curly hair on his chest. The room was silent except for the faint sound of rain outside. But even the soothing sound of rainfall couldn't change the tense look on his face.

Murali got up from the chair on seeing Inspector More and said, 'I need to discuss something important with you.'

'Is it about the call that you had mentioned?'

Murali nodded and said, 'That's the reason I called you at this late hour.'

At about one o'clock in the afternoon, someone with a gravelly voice had called the ANC headquarters and told Murali that a bulky stash of cocaine, worth Rs 25 crores, had entered the city.

A Nigerian man, who routinely transported *maal* in and out of the city, was going to deliver it to a man touted as Mumbai's cocaine king. The deal was to happen in an abandoned place near Kurla, which gave Murali the home advantage. The worth of the *maal* and the people involved in the deal made him pace the room nervously. After running his fingers through his hair several times, he told More about his plan.

'We'll be there in mufti in an hour or two to keep a close watch on them.'

'I'm wondering whether the tip-off was genuine,' More said.

'It sounded genuine to me,' Murali replied. 'If it turns out to be false, we'll kick our butts and go back home but what if it turns out to be true?'

After devising a strategy, he called for tea. When it was brought to the table, More slurped it with delight. Murali raised the teacup from the saucer to put it to his lips but couldn't as the tremor in his fingers shook the cup. He kept the cup back on the saucer, and this time he raised the saucer along with the teacup and, with great difficulty, took a sip. More noted that every time he took a sip, his teacup rattled.

'Are you OK?' More asked.

Murali couldn't say a word. For a moment he sat still and then shook himself out of his reverie and said, 'I'm fine! But sometimes I'm not able to hold things in my hand. I have been dropping things a lot lately. Seems like I'm losing my grip.'

'Too much tea makes you a bit shaky,' said More.

***

The insects were roused to action by the full moon. Old cars stripped down and reduced to their parts were piled up on both sides of the road, forming a mountainous heap. Adjacent to the lonely road was a big scrapyard surrounded by thick vegetation. One could enter the yard through its front gate or by walking through the thick vegetation. The circular yard had junk piled up on its circumference and hiding behind the junk was one of Murali's men in plain clothes. Another police officer dressed like a rag-picker was hiding near the front gate. The thick vegetation close to the scrapyard served as a good hiding place for More and Murali. A stray dog with a torn ear was standing at the centre of the scrapyard where the deal was expected to take place.

Minutes turned into hours and Murali shook his head in disgust after seeing his watch. It was late, past 11:30, and the Nigerian was expected to come with the *maal* at 11:00. Murali took a cigarette, put it to his lips and activated his walkie-talkie.

'Any update? Did you see anyone?

'I've been waiting for two hours! No sign of anyone, sir,' one of the men replied.

After a few minutes, more dogs entered the scrapyard for a midnight communion. They were barking for no reason. Irritated by the blood-sucking mosquitos, Murali stepped out of the vegetation and walked quickly towards the scrapyard, ducking behind a pile of metal. Everyone was anxiously waiting for the African to arrive. Some rustling sounds were heard but it was breeze swirling a few dry leaves. After more barking and yelping, the dogs left the scrapyard but Murali's men were waiting like hungry canines themselves to catch the drug dealers red-handed. They waited till dawn before realizing that the tip-off had been nothing but a big joke.

The next evening, Murali summoned his team for an emergency meeting in his cabin. The expression on his face was serious. With raised eyebrows and furrowed forehead, he addressed his team in a voice that demanded attention.

'To me, the tip-off call sounded too good to be true. But I don't think the informer was faking it.'

More replied with his concerns regarding the existence of a mole inside the department.

'Quite possible,' Murali replied. 'But I think we should have stopped ourselves from coming too early. We made too much noise by coming an hour early, and that might have alerted them.'

While his team was figuring out what had gone wrong, Murali felt a twitch in his left arm. It lasted for almost a minute. Then, minutes later, he felt one in his right leg. He didn't bother about it until he got a twitch in his eyelid. He felt as if some tiny alien insect had got under his skin and was playing with him by pulling his nerves and muscles. To arrest the twitching, he stretched his arms and legs and it stopped, but that was only for a brief moment. It came back with a vengeance and irritated him throughout the meeting.

After the meeting, Murali left work to get some rest. He came home before time. Surprised by his early visit, Tiger pounced on him with love and his wife looked both stunned and appalled. In all these years he had never come home before time. He reacted to their reactions with an unenthusiastic grin and went to bed only to get up very late in the morning.

***

The next day, some journalists came to Murali's cabin, trying to get some stories about the drug scene in Mumbai. When asked about the current trend in selling drugs, Murali spoke about illegal Internet pharmacies that were luring young, affluent people through social media. After talking about some of his heroic drug busts, he called for refreshments. Hot samosas and kachoris with green chutney were served. The journalists gorged on them with delight while Murali appraised them of the recent initiatives to strengthen the Anti-Narcotics force.

Murali knew how to treat journalists and how to stay in their good books. After taking charge as ACP, he had instructed his team to treat journalists with respect. They returned the favour by puffing his image in the media. He was portrayed as a fearless cop with a knack for finding and busting drug rings. Even a small move from him made news. His persona attracted authors and film personalities. Books were written with stories loosely based on his life and heroic achievements. Famous Bollywood actors met with him to study his body language so that they could play the role of a police officer with perfection. He appeared in the press and on TV almost every week. The constant media attention made him put in extra hours at work. More than fulfilling the duties of a police officer, he had to work hard to save his larger-than-life image.

A few months earlier, Murali had stopped a Toyota Qualis with a Punjab number plate, which triggered his journey to unexpected popularity. After examining the engine section, he found CNG cylinders assembled in a car running on petrol. Being well aware of the modus operandi, he ripped open the CNG cylinders and fished out 33 kg of charas worth Rs 34 lakhs. All attempts made by drug dealers to smuggle narcotics into the city failed miserably as Murali had the innate ability to stop the vehicle carrying the *maal*. His powerful nose and its smelling capability was no less than that of a sniffer dog.

After getting sound bites from Murali, the media people left his office. Late in the evening, Murali asked for samosas and coffee to be sent to his cabin as tea made him a bit shaky. He took a sip from his coffee, and his face lit up with heavenly contentment. Then he reached for a crispy samosa and dipped it in the watery tomato sauce before putting it in his mouth. He crunched it with his teeth but the trouble began when he tried to swallow it. He found it difficult to push it down his throat.

All these days trivial problems like shaky hands, jittery fingers and muscle twitches were troubling him. And now swallowing difficulty came in as a new addition. He figured that something was not right with his body. Slowly, things started to get worse like a storm that starts with a mild breeze.

***

As time went by, Murali started experiencing facial weakness involving upper and lower facial muscles. Muscular pain at certain points in his left shoulder troubled him. Was it pain or weakness? He was not able to differentiate between the two. Sometimes the aches gave him sleepless nights. His wife would give him an oil massage first thing in the morning to calm his nerves. She told him to eat foods rich in Vitamin D, and advised him to get enough sunlight by going for an early morning walk. More told him to exercise twice a day. Everyone he knew played doctor and Murali followed all the instructions religiously, but nothing worked. He finally decided to consult his family doctor.

After exchanging pleasantries, Swapnil, his doctor, checked him thoroughly and enquired about his work. 'Are you dealing with any important cases?'

'Why? What's the matter with me?'

'Nothing is wrong with you. You are stressed out! It's anxiety that is troubling you. That's why I asked about your work. You should take it easy for a few days. I'll give you some vitamin shots that will make you feel good in a week's time. Don't stress! Lighten your outlook.'

Following the doctor's advice, Murali took a break from work and tried meditation to reduce his anxiety. If anything, the twitches got worse. A shooting pain would start in his left shoulder late in the evening and it would gradually travel down to the tip of his toes. He felt as if someone were playing with his muscles and nerves and having fun. In reality, fate was playing its song using his body as a musical instrument. Murali rubbished his symptoms as general exhaustion but something inside him told him that he was suffering from an insidious disease.

Murali got three stitches on his head when he busted a rave party in Bandra. Acting on a tip-off, Murali and his team entered the party and seized cannabis and Ecstasy pills. While dragging one of the junkies out of the hotel, Murali tripped and fell on his back, injuring his head. Blood gushed from his head like a waterfall, and media people sniffing around Bandra saw him fall to the ground. The next day, the newspapers talked about the drug bust and rave party but not about his fall. His good relationship with the media kept him away from all kinds of negative publicity. Tripping and falling was no big deal. But the underlying cause of his fall was something he couldn't ignore. Sometimes his legs felt like jelly and went numb. Symptoms like leg pain and numbness called for caution and his doctor told him to consult a neurologist.

***

Murali felt that he had no control over his body and it behaved as if it had a mind of its own. Something inside him was shutting down his nervous system, something invisible. His fasciculations had become constant. People who looked at him from a distance couldn't see anything wrong with him, but people close to him told him that he was showing signs of weakness and fatigue. His gym trainer had to help him lift weights and told him categorically that he had lost stamina. His biceps and triceps were losing their definition. His symptoms when viewed singly posed no threat, but collectively, they made a serious impact.

Murali started getting leg cramps while working in his office. Inspector More played doctor and told him to drink more water. His wife told him to consume a healthy diet with plenty of fresh fruits and vegetables. To deal with frequent muscle cramps, he was injected with potassium and magnesium solutions. He met a nutritionist and got himself a diet chart. He gorged on protein-rich food. He did all that he could to gain muscle strength. But the symptoms paid no heed to his lifestyle changes. Some days he felt alright, but some days he felt drained and jaded.

One fine day, frustrated by his clumsiness, Murali grabbed his gun and walked to the nearby police training centre to test his shooting and trigger control skills. He took his position and aimed at the bullseye. His eyes scanned the black dots. His heart raced. His arms quivered a bit, but he quickly regained his posture. 'Come on, Murali,' he encouraged himself, and placed his finger on the trigger. He stared at the target board and began to put pressure on the trigger. With unrelenting confidence he fired ten quick shots. To his surprise, all the bullets missed the bullseye, missed the concentric circles, missed the target board, and made ten gaping holes in the metal frame that supported the board. At that moment, Murali decided that he has to meet Dr Shyam as soon as possible.

***

Monsoon rains bade farewell and gave way to winter. Outside, the scene was foggy and gloomy. Poor people were burning junk to keep themselves warm. After drinking his hot *chai*, Murali stood near the window of his cabin and looked down at the street. Then he diverted his gaze towards the trophy shelf. His prized possessions were neatly stacked inside a glass cupboard. A few years earlier IIT Bombay had awarded him a PhD degree for his research on drug abuse. His medals and trophies spoke of his bravery. He had bagged three President's Police Medals for distinguished service. In 2001, he was adjudged "Super Cop" by the Mumbai Police Circle and informally called "Sherlock Holmes" of Mumbai for his investigative capabilities. During his tenure as Sub-Inspector of Police in 1996, he had been instrumental in solving several cold cases and murders. Apart from being a Super Cop, several shields displayed his capabilities in various sporting activities such as running, swimming, shooting and cycling. The sight of the cups, medals, shields, trophies and framed certificates lifted his mood, and he felt better.

Suddenly, he heard a voice. 'Sir, we have an appointment at Mantralaya,' said More, a serious look on his face. For a moment, Murali stood motionless. He was so shocked by what he could do before and what he could do now. His symptoms had drained the life from him. More noticed that his arms had started to thin, and his brawny body had lost its shape. He asked the usual questions: 'How are you doing today? How's your health?' That was all anyone had to say to Murali.

'We need to get going,' said Murali and dug his hands into his pockets to get the jeep key. When they were about to leave, the telephone trilled.

Murali received the call and heard a raspy voice. It was another tip-off. After 55 seconds of talking, the caller hung up. Murali's face turned ecstatic and seeing his reaction, Inspector More enquired about the call.

'The Nigerian is still roaming with the *maal*. The cocaine worth 25 crore rupees has still not reached its buyer. This is another chance for us to get it right!' said Murali.

'Did he say anything else? I heard you asking him about place and time … Which place? Is it Kurla again?' asked More.

'No, Thane.'

What time?'

'Tomorrow at 00:45 hours. I'm pretty sure it's not a hoax.'

'How can you be so sure?'

'He's my trusted informant. I've known him for a long time. This time we'll catch them red-handed.'

***

It was a moonless night and the sky was empty with no stars to fill the dark firmament. The road beside the lake was deserted. Street lights that ran across the deserted road, planted at regular intervals, were poorly lit. A line of tall trees on both sides of the lane added to the poor visibility. A dilapidated building stood near the lake, touching the deserted road, and next to the building stood an abandoned temple. Everything was bathed in a dull yellow. The chirping of crickets irritated Murali more than the tiny mosquitos that were hovering around him, waiting to suck his blood. Inspector More and his subordinate, dressed in mufti, were hiding behind the bushes near the lake. Hiding behind the temple wall, Murali activated his walkie-talkie and spoke to More in a hush-hush voice, informing him of his position.

Minutes passed, the chirping of crickets grew louder, and to his horror, Murali felt a moving pain in his right leg. Unable to stand, he supported himself using the wall, and sat with a thud on the ground. He shook his head a few times in an attempt to get his mind back to the present situation. Sometimes pain blanked his mind and made him lose concentration and focus.

Suddenly, from somewhere near the temple, More heard a faint cry. He blanked his mind and ignored the faint cry as something nugatory. Minutes later, he heard it again. This time he readied himself with a gun and told his subordinate to take a look. In spite of being near the temple, Murali was not able to hear the cry. Pain along with the growing sound of crickets crippled his senses.

More's subordinate, a lanky young man, emerged out of the bushes like a jungle animal and ambled towards the source of the cry. When he reached the threshold of the temple, he saw a torch lying on the ground. Next to the torch was a dark figure lying motionless. He took the torch and shone it on the figure. To his horror, he saw a Nigerian man with a bloodied face. The faint cry that he had made a while back had been his last. His eyeballs were fixed and unblinking. Beads of saliva glistened on his lips and his thick beard gave him a rugged look. A revolver was lying next to him. Blood dotted his white shirt. Something lying on the dead man's chest caught his attention. He leaned down for a closer look and saw several packets filled with cocaine. To verify his assumption, he took one packet from the lot and sniffed it deeply. After smelling the *maal*, he signalled to More to join him.

Meanwhile, Murali was trying to divert his mind from his leg pain, when, suddenly, he saw someone standing, hiding behind the temple wall. Without wasting a second, he got up, slow-walked towards the dark figure, gripped his gun, and pointed it at the back of his head and said, 'Hands up, don't try to do anything stupid.'

***

The next day, when Murali arrived at the station, Inspector More was looking at the photographs of the dead Nigerian, trying to find a match using the Image Matching software to see if he existed in their database. 'The software is not giving me any positive results. I think he's a new mule and the packets we found were leftovers, not even worth 50,000,' said Inspector More.

'Tell me your first thoughts on the crime scene,' said Murali.

'Seems like a drug deal gone bad,' said More, his voice low-pitched and his face etched with deep dejection.

'The tip-off was genuine; we just got the timings wrong,' sighed Murali. 'The *maal* must have reached its owner. We have to trace the cocaine as soon as possible. Let's get started and proceed with what we have in hand. First, I'll interrogate and get the truth out of our suspect.'

More took a lathi in his hand, got him out of the cell and started his interrogation.

'Did he say anything?' he asked one of his subordinates.

'No, sir.'

'What is your full name?'

'Peter Thomas.'

'Do you have a family?'

'No.'

'Father?'

'He's no more; he died.'

'Mother?'

'She died too.'

'So, you are a loner eh?'

'Yes.'

'What do you know about the African?'

He kept mum.

Murali grilled him with questions on the cocaine packets for which he got no satisfactory answers. Late in the evening, he got a call and someone on the other end confirmed his appointment with the neurologist.

***

It was evident that something was wrong with his nerves and muscles. An extreme tiredness plagued him, and after a long wait, Dr Shyam – Mumbai's best neurologist – called Murali into his clinic. With a serious look on his face, he examined Murali and asked about his symptoms. Murali told him about all the symptoms he was suffering from.

'Twitching, cramps, shaky hands, jittery fingers, difficulty swallowing, muscle weakness, tiredness, fatigue and sometimes sharp pain in arms and legs at night. Let's see … ' Dr Shyam paused to think.

Meanwhile, Murali browsed his clinic and saw the nameplate on his table. A host of degrees attached to his name gave him confidence. A complex chart depicting the human nervous system was nailed to the wall.

'What do you actually feel? Do you feel pain?' the doctor asked.

Murali couldn't find a word to describe what he was going through as the word 'pain' seemed inappropriate to him.

'I'm not feeling any pain, like, physical pain,' Murali replied. 'It's like someone sitting inside me and draining all my energy. Just like water spiralling and draining down the hole.'

In order to test his reflexes, Dr Shyam conducted a thorough neurological physical examination with a help of a reflex hammer. He struck the hammer onto his tendons to elicit a reflex. Murali reacted positively.

'You've got great reflexes!' the doctor said. That made Murali happy, if only for a few minutes. After asking a few close-ended questions about his health, the doctor got up and made his way across the room to a glass shelf stocked with books. He reached for the bottom-most shelf, and referred to some books before taking his next course of action.

'How long have you been having these symptoms?'

'Four weeks!'

'I don't see any major problem but we need to get a few things scanned. Give this paper to the front desk. I'll see you in a week's time,' he said and trilled the bell to call for the next patient.

Murali couldn't understand his handwriting and asked the man sitting at the front desk for an explanation. His reply made Murali's heart thump with fear and the muscles in his body twitched faster than normal.

'We need to do a brain scan as soon as possible.'

***

Murali was asked to remove any objects containing metal such as jewellery and he was told to come on an empty stomach. He was told to wear hospital clothes: a loose shirt and pyjamas. After wearing them, he glanced at the mirror; the loose clothes made him look like a cancer patient. Then he was told to lie flat on a scanning table. A plastic coil was placed around his head. The technician dutifully slid the table into the doughnut-shaped tunnel and after a few seconds, everything went dark. Then he could see colourful worm-like creatures curling up and vanishing without a trace. A pair of headphones with a device was given to him. Silence engulfed the room, but when Murali activated the music system, the eerie silence was replaced by metallic beats. The metallic beats were further replaced by a persistent, irritating noise from the MRI machine and he felt as if someone were hitting his head with a hammer. It was a painful process as Murali felt claustrophobic and it took 45 minutes for the machine to capture the detailed images of his brain and brain stem. The resulting output was a clear, cross-sectional black and white image of his brain which looked like a big walnut.

The scan came out clean. Tests were done to check his kidneys and they were found to be healthy. His liver was clean and healthy. His lungs were as clear as crystal. His cardiac health was good. After examining the functions of his vital organs, Dr Shyam shook his head. 'There's nothing wrong with you,' he said. But for Murali, every day was a surprise. New symptoms continued to invade his body. Dr Shyam wanted to analyze his spinal fluid before coming to any conclusions. Murali was advised to keep a diary of his symptoms.

***

Murali went to Lilavathi and met a young woman who lectured him on spinal fluid before giving him a hospital gown. She ushered him to a technician who told him to lie on his side with his legs and hips flexed up towards his chest like a baby in its mother's womb. After numbing the target area of his back, the technician inserted a needle in his lower back, between two vertebrae, to enter the space where the fluid is contained. Then he sucked the fluid out of his body and Murali felt as if someone were sucking the life out of him and showing him the door to death.

The fluid was made to drip into the vial at its own pace and after collecting it into a series of two or three vials, the technician removed the needle and covered the punctured area with a bandage.

'It's over buddy!' the technician said. 'Just lie flat on your back for some time and relax! Don't forget to drink a lot of water. Your punctured area may be sore for a day or two and you might experience dizziness or headaches. Drink coffee or tea first thing in the morning. Tell your wife to keep an eye on the punctured area. It should be monitored for signs of infection like redness, swelling or pus. Your test results will be ready in a week's time.'

Murali was told to take complete rest and without wasting too much time, he drove home and slept the sleep of the dead for the first time in his life.

***

Murali's boss, the Deputy Commissioner of Police, Mr Parkar, approved his sabbatical leave. Weakness and loss of strength in his arms made him feel like a vegetable and rendered him incapable of lifting or moving objects. Thoughts about death and impermanence clouded his mind. The media couldn't stop commenting on his absence. At home, his wife, servants, and even his dog viewed him as someone who was suffering a terminal illness. He started to look like a skeleton clothed in skin. Muscle loss in his arms and legs made them look like a pair of sticks attached to a scrawny body. He browsed the photos of his past days and realized that he no longer resembled a fit officer.

After seeing his symptom diary, Dr Shyam decided to go for some blood and urine tests to check for the enzyme creatine kinase, which leaks out of damaged muscle. All his fluids were collected for laboratory analysis. More than the symptoms, the tests to find the root cause of the symptoms stressed Murali out. Next on the list was a nerve conduction study.

Before the procedure, the technician gave him a hospital gown and some encouraging words, saying everything would be alright but he administered a mild electric current into his body. A pair of electrodes were attached to his arm to record the impulse. The current nudged his brain and probed his nerves. The resulting output was complex: a series of numbers and waves displayed on a small monitor. When Murali asked the technician about the test, he replied with some names of nerve diseases that could be detected but everything sounded like gibberish to Murali. The study had no serious after effects on him, but it left him a bit shaky.

Evening walks with his wife and Tiger got him out of his gloomy state but sometimes while walking he had to drag his feet along the ground and that's when things started to get a bit more serious. In spite of taking sleeping pills he had trouble falling asleep at night, was distracted by the faintest sound, and at times, he sat up in bed at the middle of the night, staring through the dark. Lack of sleep had put him into a sort of stupor, and he felt groggy and sluggish during the day.

Murali's transformation from a burly cop to a puny patient pushed him into depression. His mind was full of unpleasant thoughts. *Am I suffering from a terminal disease? What will happen to me in a month's time? Will I die? Who will take care of my wife? What's wrong with me? Why don't the doctors have a clue about what's happening? Is my nervous system fucked up?* The ranting in his mind went on and on. Shock coupled with nervousness shook him on the inside. Finally, he was told he could undergo another test that might possibly throw some light on his mysterious illness.

'Let's do an Electromyogram and back it up with a nerve conduction study,' the doctor said. 'That will give us a clear picture.' When Murali asked some of his friends, they said, 'It's like paying money to undergo torture!'

***

Murali, sitting in Lilavati Hospital with his wife, saw the technician who looked like a dictator running a torture chamber. He asked him about the severity of the shock waves. The technician told him not to anticipate anything and instructed him to remove his shirt. Ribs peeped through his skin, wanting to be freed. Searching for some flesh in his bony arms and shoulders, the technician started inserting the needles, one by one, slowly, and methodically. Within minutes he was pricked by several needles in his arms and shoulders. The needles felt like pin pricks but the shocks that followed and flowed through the needles into his system struck him like lightning. Initially, he was told to tighten his arms and move his shoulders to record muscle activity, but the shocking part came much later in the form of electric shocks.

After administering a series of mild shocks, the technician gradually increased the intensity, and when it reached its maximum permissible level, Murali jolted and yelled like a lunatic. Intense pain overtook him and made him weary. It was like a battle between two sources of pain: an external pain induced to examine an internal pain.

'It's over!' the technician said after pricking and shocking him for 50 long minutes, and Murali, who had been waiting to hear these words, heaved a sigh of relief.

The output of Electromyogram coupled with the study was a heady mix of logic, mathematics and graphs. A bunch of wavy and spiky lines sprinkled with numbers perplexed Murali. The test left him in more pain than before and the piercing caused mauve–blue spots on his arms and legs. All his results were collected and sent to Dr Shyam for his analysis. 'In a week's time, with all these data, I should be able to come up with an accurate medical diagnosis,' he said. Murali had no choice but to wait for things to unfold.

***

The week that led Murali to the judgement day moved at a snail's pace. Negative thoughts crowded his mind like jostling passengers in a Mumbai local. He refrained from meeting people and sat at home pondering death, the afterlife and other philosophical thoughts.

Surprisingly, on D-Day, the twitching in his arms and legs came to a halt and all the negative emotions that had been bubbling inside him took a break. His wife told him to visit the nearby Ganesh temple before meeting Dr Shyam, who was waiting to write his fate.

The temple was crowded. Murali folded his hands in a namaste before the elephant god and prayed for the continuity of his life. Being pious and going to temples had never been his way of dealing with tough situations but the fear of death propelled him towards faith. The priest blessed him and applied a streak of sacred white ash on his forehead.

Murali reached the clinic before time and enquired about Dr Shyam. 'He'll see you in another five minutes,' said the lady at the front desk. Those five minutes almost killed him, and when his turn came, he nervously walked into Shyam's cabin and greeted him, his voice cracking with emotion when he spoke. He felt clammy, a bit shaky all of a sudden it was as if a tremor had hit him. He took a series of deep breaths that calmed his thumping heart.

'Why don't you sit there?' said Dr Shyam, pointing to the chair. It took some time for him to settle down and he sat facing Shyam, his knuckles drumming the table. To beat his anxiety, Shyam got him a glass of water. After small-talking with Murali for a few minutes, he fished out his report and wore glasses to read them.

After blinking his eyes a few times, Dr Shyam cleared his throat and gave a lengthy commentary on Murali's health. 'I know you've been a tough guy all your life! I've read about your actions in the newspapers. Handling crooks and rogues is not an easy job. You have a strong heart! That's why I'm going to give it to you straight without beating around the bush. I believe you are suffering from a rare neurodegenerative disease. To put it in simple terms, your muscles and nerves are slowly dying. Unfortunately, the disease that you are suffering from is not completely understood; it's called Amyotrophic lateral sclerosis – ALS or Lou Gehrig's disease. The cause of ALS is not known. Research says that 5 to 10% of people suffering from ALS inherit the disease from their family. In your case, seeing your family history, I don't think it's familial. Another disease that closely mimics ALS is Hirayama disease, but it is prevalent only in Japan. The virus or bug has randomly selected you from a batch of 10,00,000 people and that's quite unfortunate! Moreover, it's a difficult disease to diagnose, and till date, there is no one test or procedure to single out ALS. I concluded it by using the process of elimination and I also got a second opinion from an ALS expert. I can prescribe some medicine that will delay your symptoms but there's no way to stop or reverse the effects of ALS. Soon you'll need a cane to walk but don't lose hope. We'll try our best, and then leave all the rest to God.'

After hearing him out, Murali jumped the gun and asked a practical question with a sombre expression on his face. 'How much time do I have?'

Dr Shyam gave no reply as he looked around, avoiding eye contact. A wave of compassion swelled in him and he momentarily thought that he should not talk about Murali's inevitable end.

But Murali pressed for an answer by asking the question again. 'How much time do I have?'

Dr Shyam had no choice but to answer him, 'Two years or maybe three, I can't say for sure. Lucky patients live five years or more; some live more than ten years after diagnosis! Your initial symptoms may be a bit subtle, but over time, you might experience difficulty in moving, swallowing, speaking or forming words. I don't mean to scare you, but that's what happens to people with ALS. As the disease progresses, all voluntary muscle movements will be affected. Involuntary muscle movements are generally spared, so you won't have problems with the stomach, intestines or digestion. Things get worse when the disease hits the respiratory system. As

ALS weakens the muscles involved with breathing, you may have to pump in more energy to breathe. But you should thank your stars because this disease does not usually affect your ability to think and it spares the sense of sight, touch, taste, hearing and smell.'

Murali spoke sarcastically. 'To sum it up, you say I have this unfathomable illness – and no one knows where it comes from, no one knows what causes it, no one knows how to treat it and no one knows how to make it go away. And you say my senses will remain intact, but what's the point? It's like my tongue can taste but my throat can't swallow; I can touch but I cannot grab or lift; I can hear but I cannot respond; I can smell but I cannot eat, and I can see it all happening but I won't be able to do anything about it. That's cruel! That's fucking cruel!'

Dr Shyam straightened up and spoke words of hope. 'Don't worry! Research to find a cure for ALS is in full swing. Americans are putting a lot of money into accelerating the development of an effective treatment. Every day scientists are getting closer and closer to finding a cure. Clinical trials to cure Motor Neuron Disease is underway and they are trying to determine whether stem cell treatment can improve the lives of ALS patients. There are even research teams studying neurodegeneration and they are trying to find out why nerve cells die. So you'll have to just hold on … Be positive … Soon, we'll hit on something absolutely new, and it's just a matter of time before we come up with a cure for ALS. You should be … '

Murali broke off the speech as the encouraging discourse was of no help to him. With a face as serious as a philosopher he asked Dr Shyam a basic question about his illness as if they had been talking about the wrong subject all this while. 'What's the name of the disease? AL . . . What? Could you please repeat it?'

'ALS – Amyotrophic lateral sclerosis.'

***

It took some time for the bad news to sink into Murali. The shock was not immediately felt; it slowly seeped into his being like alcohol and clouded his mind. He walked out of Dr Shyam's clinic in a daze. Intense sorrow made him walk in a random direction, like a zombie. As usual, his legs refused to support him and he couldn't even walk half a kilometre at a stretch. He entered a shopping mall for a change of scenery. Shock, anger, fear, denial, helplessness, sadness, frustration and a dozen other emotions warred inside him. To think things through with a calm mind he entered a Starbucks coffee shop and ordered an espresso. Within minutes, the waiter approached him and placed his cup on the table.

'Can I get you something to eat?' the waiter asked Murali.

'No, thank you,' he said, and after a few sips of espresso his mind started its ranting again.

Why me? Why choose me from a lot of 10,00,000 people? I don't want to die young … Is it my karma? Can I change my karma? Why should I suffer? Is there really something like cause and effect? I save people from becoming drug addicts … I'm useful to society … I should have been rewarded for my past actions and present doings … not punished … Can someone cure my disease? Why do bad things happen to good people? I will fight …

His angry, impassioned thoughts were interrupted when the waiter reappeared with the bill. He paid and came out of the shop, and looked at the people around him. Young couples, families, children and older people were shopping, going up and down the escalator. Some people were quite animated;

others were taking it easy, sipping cool drinks and eating pizza. He observed every activity; all of it seemed pointless, like chasing the wind. The sting of death took away his delight in being alive and turned every event, even time, into meaningless fiction.

Occasionally, the time was punctuated with moments of clarity that gave him faith and courage, but the overwhelming question, "Why me?" filled his heart with hatred and dejection. Murali wanted to cry like an infant. He couldn't swallow the karma pill and the idea that karma of past life affects the present life. He looked around the mall again, trying to see whether there was anything worthy of being noticed. Nothing interested him. So he left the mall and took a taxi home.

Doing trivial everyday activities turned out to be a big challenge for him. The lift in his building refused to work and he had no option but to take the stairs. It took him some time to climb to his apartment. ALS was slowly draining the life from his legs. It took double the time for him to unlock the door and let himself in. His wife was standing in the living room, waiting for him anxiously. Tiger came running to him and sniffed him wildly. That was his way of asking what had happened at the clinic. Murali tried his best to talk but he couldn't form any words as he was in a state of desolation. Seeing him, his wife understood things quickly. She saw right away the grief etched on his face, and a sense of foreboding. Finally, when Murali told her about his condition she burst into tears. Seeing her cry, Tiger nervously paced the room. It took a while for things to settle down. His wife convinced him to try Ayurveda or Siddha or Unani but a little research cleared the fact that there was no cure for ALS and traditional Indian medicines were unable to cure MND. Conversation between the two continued, dwelling on the immediate steps to be taken to get Murali out of the stranglehold of ALS. Every sentence that his wife uttered ended with a question mark and every answer that he gave continued endlessly without a full stop. After a while, their talking ceased, and they looked at each other with tired eyes. Even Tiger stopped pacing and snuggled quietly under the sofa. The room fell silent except for the tick-tock coming from the clock that seemed to convey an important message to Murali. Tick-tock, tick-tock, your days are numbered. Tick-tock, tick-tock, you are slowly being pitched towards death. Tick-tock, tick-tock, your time is running out.

The eerie quiet was interrupted by a ringing telephone. Murali was in no mood to talk but the phone trilled continuously, wanting to be picked up. He answered the call with a low-pitched, lifeless "hello". It was Inspector More on the other end.

'Peter has escaped!'

'What the fuck are you taking about? How did this happen?'

'He complained of some kidney problem and we had him admitted to Vashi Civic hospital following the doctor's advice. We kept an eye on him but he was too fast for us. He escaped through the bathroom window. It was not a random act of intelligence but a part of a well-thought-out plan. A Toyota was standing near the hospital building to pick him up. We couldn't see the number plate and the car vanished.'

'He was my prize catch, and you guys couldn't keep him in?' exclaimed Murali. 'When did this happen?'

***

His wife's uncle's friend introduced Murali to one of his kind: a man in his forties diagnosed with ALS. Murali regarded him as a species from another planet because he was suffering from a rare type of ALS, Type20, yet he spoke about beating the disease. When asked for his survival techniques, he gave Murali some pointers on how to go about the task.

- Take RILUTEK tablets – 50mg every 12 hours. It will slow down the progression of the disease. If you are lucky you won't suffer any side effects.
- Do meditation. One hour in the morning and one in the evening. That will calm your mind.
- Accept the disease. This will put a lot of negative emotions to rest and will give rise to positive emotions.
- Understand the mind–body connection. A healthy body leads to a healthy mind and vice versa. Don't think too much.
- Exercise for one hour every day, thirty minutes in the morning and thirty minutes in the evening. Do squats to strengthen your buttocks and thighs. One-arm row to strengthen upper and middle back and shoulders. Push-ups for chest, abdominals, shoulders and arms. Shoulder press for shoulders and arms. Biceps curls for biceps. Kick-backs for triceps.
- If possible, do yoga. Do simple asanas to improve flexibility and balance. It will make your body supple. Some breathing techniques may maximize lung function.
- Don't stay idle. The disease hits you harder if you are idle. Keep your mind and body occupied.
- What you eat defines you! You need good nutrition to lead a quality life. Avoid sugar and dairy products. I suggest you have a caveman's diet. Eat fruits. Snack on nuts. Muscles need protein, so eat meat. Eat as many vegetables as you want. Look for fish and

omega-3-rich eggs. Eat things with wings – chicken, duck and hen. Tell your wife to use olive oil or coconut oil for cooking. A good diet won't cure ALS but it will give you strength to fight the disease.

- Find ways to conserve energy. ALS kills you by sapping your energy.
- Smoke cannabis. It protects the nervous system when smoked in moderation. Not highly recommended.
- Don't lose weight. Try to consume more calories.
- Anxiety and depression can kill you faster than ALS. Avoid them.
- Be positive. Don't lose hope. Surround yourself with happy and optimistic people.
- Believe in God. Believe in miracles, because they do happen.

Murali followed his instructions diligently for a couple of weeks but nothing happened. There were no visible signs of improvement except for the fact that regular exercise and yoga strengthened his legs. Herbs, green smoothies and other natural remedies proved fruitless. His wife made him gobble concoctions made of medicinal leaves but the symptoms paid no heed to her faith in Ayurveda. On the contrary, the symptoms hopped on to the next stage, as if someone had pressed the fast-forward button to bring him closer to death.

A week or so passed, and the disease shocked him with new warning signs. One fine morning, to alleviate his anxiety, his wife gave him tomato soup. While his tongue slurped the soup with delight, his throat refused to ingest it. After finishing his tomato soup with great difficulty he asked her to bring fruit salad. To maintain good nutrition, she served him fresh salad prepared using nine different fruits and disappeared into the kitchen to get herself some coffee. When she came out of the kitchen, she saw him opening and closing his mouth like a fish. Murali was trying to talk but he couldn't form any words. After some time, things cleared up, words came out, but it sounded like gibberish. He experienced a sudden onset of speech impairment. He spoke like an old drunkard; his words were slurred and clumsy. As time went by, he had multiple episodes of slurred speech. As his speech continued to deteriorate, his wife took him to a speech therapist. The speech–language pathologist got him a microphone and amplifier to project his voice. Murali was told to learn three-syllable and four-syllable phrases for effective communication and his wife was told to learn lip reading. He felt like an immature baby.

Weakness in the muscles of his tongue was followed by swallowing and chewing difficulty. Liquids made him cough, even water. Small activities like chewing food exhausted him. Dry, crunchy food items were a no-no. Mealtimes became lengthy. Sometimes, lassitude reduced his ability to finish his meal and that resulted in weight loss and malnutrition. Fatigue plagued him time and again. His jaws quivered while yawning. At night, he sometimes experienced breathlessness. Every morning, he longed for evening to come and every evening, he wanted to get to the end of the day.

Time passed, and Murali's health deteriorated further. His wife took him to Dr Shyam and asked the same questions again and again.

'Will he recover?'

'Can you reverse ALS?'

'What should I do if he develops severe side effects?'

'Do you have any specialized treatment for ALS?'

'What research is being done on ALS?'

'Is it a limb-onset or bulbar-onset?'

'Can he travel?'

'How much should he exercise?'

'How do ALS patients die? Do they choke?'

She knew the answers to most of these questions but she couldn't quell her desperation. Dr Shyam gave her the same old answers. Another symptom, though trivial, made Murali change his clothes up to five times a day because he drooled down the front of his shirts. Overflow of saliva in his mouth irritated him. He had to carry a napkin all the time and he shied away from social events. Frequent blood tests made him weary and then there were yellow pills, green pills and pills of all other colours that he swallowed to treat his secondary conditions like stomach pain, low fever and dry cough. His wife did all that she could to nurse him to health but her efforts were in vain.

He couldn't brush his teeth. He lost his ability to wash and feed himself. He could no longer drive his car. He couldn't hold his gun steadily. He tried to put on his police uniform but he couldn't button the shirt as he was having problems with his fingers. He couldn't shave and the thick hair on his face made him look sick. He couldn't write or put down his signature. He couldn't say to his wife the three sweet words that reside in the soul of every loving heart: I love you.

***

Murali went Google-crazy and browsed sites that offered him ALS cures, but all of them turned out to be bogus. His medical expenses were burning a hole in his pocket. Every week, he visited a bunch of specialists: physical therapist, occupational therapist, speech language pathologist, dietician, pulmonologist and a couple of others who answered his questions and offered help. Antidepressant and anti-anxiety medications plagued him with minor side effects like stomach upsets, dizziness and drowsiness. He was injected with botulinum toxin and multivitamins on a regular basis, and sometimes he stayed at the hospital overnight to deal with his breathing problems. Sometimes, a wave of intense emotions swept over him in a short period of time, making him laugh and cry in quick succession. He tried his best to throw off the disease with his positive attitude but the psychological impact of ALS was so overwhelming that it buried all the optimism in him.

'The muscle strength of your legs seems to be improving,' said Dr Shyam. His words came as a ray of hope in the midst of the despondency that had settled on him after months of ineffective treatment. Murali felt better but his bulbar symptoms such as dysphagia and dysarthria were speeding up. He spent the afternoons watching TV, trying to lose himself in a movie or a song but sometimes, his behaviour was weird. He laughed uncontrollably while watching a song with a lot of pathos and he cried incessantly when they showed scenes of happiness and glee.

That's when his wife called the clinical psychologist who visited him every week to check on his emotional well-being. Bouts of laughter and crying were common among people with bulbar issues, he said.

Everything that Murali did felt like a strenuous exercise; walking, talking, taking a bath, opening the door, wearing clothes and even breathing exhausted him. He smoked marijuana to deal with muscle spasms though Dr Shyam advised him not to use such things. What irony! A narcotics officer smoking weed!

To cope with his emotional turbulence he watched a lot of YouTube videos about ALS. Some videos gave him hope and encouraged him to fight. Some videos freaked him out but two of them in particular made him re-evaluate his health. The first showed a machine feeding a man. The camera zoomed and revealed a pen-sized hole in his belly that acted like a window into his stomach through which solids and liquids were ingested with a help of a tube. The video was titled *Final Stages of ALS.*

In another disturbing video, Murali saw a man confined to his wheel chair. The camera zoomed and focussed its gaze on a tube inserted into his windpipe through the throat and the other end of the tube was connected to a breathing machine. The patient was breathing through the machine. In fact, the machine was breathing for him. After seeing this series of dreadful videos, Murali's mind was filled with suicidal thoughts for the first time in his life.

One fine morning, Murali woke up to find that his body was dying in parts. His shoulders were frozen to the spot, and he couldn't move them. While walking he tried to swing his arms but he couldn't get any momentum. His arms were pinned to his sides.

A week later, his fingers stopped working, except for his right thumb. When he was too weary to speak he communicated with his wife by typing words on his cell phone. The idea of staying alive with the help of machines scared him. He wanted to discuss the immediate next steps with Dr Shyam before letting the machines take over his eating and breathing.

***

'Caaaaaan you do soooomeething to halt myyyyyyyy symptomssssssss ...' Murali slurred. His wife wiped his saliva with a tissue. The sight of phlegm and saliva pooling in his mouth disturbed Dr Shyam but he maintained his calm. A middle-aged woman emerged, holding a trumpet-like gadget in her hands, and sat next to Shyam.

'Meet Dr Nirupama, she's our pulmonary specialist,' said Dr Shyam. 'She'll test your breathing capability.' Wasting no time, Dr Nirupama sprang into action and motioned to Murali to join her in another room. He sat cross-legged across the table from her, and looked at her nervously as she placed a clip on his nose. There was tension in the air. He took a deep breath and exhaled through his mouth into a computer using the trumpet-like equipment. He did this several times and the results were available on the computer screen.

When Murali asked her about the results she threw acronyms like FVC, TLC and a couple of others that went over his head. The output was a bunch of numbers and graphs. She printed out the readings, laid her conclusions before Dr Shyam and made her way out of the clinic.

After deciphering the readings, Dr Shyam said, 'Murali, breathing will soon be a day-to-day battle for you. Your lungs are fine but the muscles that move the air in and out are slowly dying. You may need a ventilator soon. I may sound a little uncouth telling you this ... but ... I advise you to get your legal and financial matters sorted.'

After hearing him say those words, Murali gathered all the strength that was left in him, and replied in a terrifying bawl. 'I don't want to die! Can you do something?'

Dr Shyam pacified him and launched into a lengthy monologue. 'Researchers are now working on things at the cellular level. Before I get into the details, you should know some stem cell basics: they are like master cells – the cell of all cells and they can turn into anything. You can try your luck with stem cell therapy but it's an experimental treatment and could cost you your health, even your life. It's a risky affair! It's like entering a dark alley. Almost all countries are into stem cell tourism to make money but I am not a fan of this therapy. It cashes in on your desperation and makes you spend a lot of money on an unproven treatment. One of my patients, a 36-year-old male, a family man like you, was suffering from MND. He knew that he had only a few months to live and he agreed to go through with the procedure. He went to America and the doctors operated on him for more than five hours. They sucked healthy stem cells from his body through a needle, derived new motor neuron cells from them, and injected the new cells back into his system. Four days after the operation, his immune system rejected the new cells. His white blood cell count fell drastically, leaving him susceptible to all kinds of diseases. He was put in a quarantined room and visitors were not permitted to enter the room without donning gloves and masks. Immunosuppressant drugs made him sick. Antibiotics couldn't keep the infections at bay. Nothing worked. He died about four months after the stem cell treatment.

'But there are always exceptions to every story. Who knows, it might work for you! Miracles do happen! I know an ALS expert in America who treats many patients and has a lot of experience in this field. I can talk to him about your case. Let me know if you're OK with it. The ... '

'As a last resort, let'ssss giveeeeee it a tryyyyyyy!' said Murali. There was anxiety in his voice.

Dr Shyam continued as if he hadn't been interrupted. 'The problem is, though ALS is pretty common in India, awareness of the disease is almost zero. Statistics says that 3 lakh people die of ALS every year in India and the Madras type of ALS that causes deafness has been prevalent in southern cities since 1970, and yet many Indians don't know anything about MND and its variants. With more than 200 potential treatments being considered for ALS in the US today, I think going to Pennsylvania for treatment makes sense, but it's a big decision! I will consult with Dr Richard and share your files with him. He's a good friend and has been an investigator for several ALS clinical trials at Penn ALS centre in Pennsylvania.'

'I'm reaaaaady to travelllll; let's exhaust all optionssssss!' slurred Murali in a sarcastic tone of voice.

'Can he travel?' his wife asked.

'Yes,' said Dr Shyam. 'His legs are fine but his bulbar symptoms are speeding up. We have to take steps before it becomes worse.'

'I don't wanttttt a hole in my bellyyyyyy to eat and a hole in myyyyyy throat to breatheeeee,' said Murali. Tears were streaming down his cheeks. Dr Shyam comforted him, said some encouraging words and handed him a brochure on Penn ALS centre.

***

Murali felt like a baby again, an ailing baby who had to be cared for, fed and nurtured. Most of the time he was wallowing in self-pity. The day that Murali had dreaded came swiftly. His wife dressed him in police uniform and helped him put on his boots. He took a walking stick with him, because a bad fall could complicate matters further. A taxi was waiting for them. She assisted him into the taxi as he was a bit unsteady on his feet and told the driver to take them to Cuffe Parade. The taxi smelled of stale cigarettes and the odour grew on him. Finally, unable to bear the stench any longer, he signalled to his wife to lower the glass and he stared out of the window. His wife warned him about the soot in the air and he realized how vulnerable he was to everything that surrounded him. The taxi sped past the narrow streets of Kurla and headed towards the ANC headquarters.

The stage was set for a tearful farewell and a large group of ANC police officers was gathered in the conference room. Murali appeared with his wife by his side and walked towards the podium. His wife helped him to a chair on the stage and he signalled to her to start. She cleared her throat and spoke his words.

'I can't hold a gun anymore. For that matter, I can't even hold a pencil. I can't catch anybody and I can't threaten anyone with my voice. My soul is intact but my body is slowly dying. I'm suffering from a neurological disease that causes muscle weakness and paralysis. I find it is no longer possible for me to continue my duties as a police officer. The cop in me is trapped inside my body. It is with a heavy heart that I leave the position I assumed many years ago. I don't want to make this sound like a farewell speech by saying thank you and goodbye. I would like to come back some day. And I don't want to leave anything incomplete on my desk before I go. You guys have to catch Peter! Search and catch him! I'll then be a happy man.'

***

Murali's wife called her cousins in New York, briefed them on his ill-health and arranged for her and Murali to stay at their place. Before taking the plunge, Murali wanted to have a chat with Dr Richard. Shyam arranged for a video conference and Dr Richard's words gave him a glimmer of hope.

'Every day we are learning something new about ALS and neurodegeneration. If you watch the destruction of motor neuron cells under an electron microscope, you'll go crazy! It's like a war! Rogue cells follow military tactics to attack good cells. So many things go haywire in your body to give you ALS. Neurodegeneration is extremely complicated, more complicated than vector algebra. Our body has an internal quality control mechanism to weed out defective cells and proteins like Six Sigma process. In ALS, the quality check fails, Six Sigma goes for a toss and defective proteins accumulate, contributing to the disease.

'The biology behind ALS keeps changing every day. To put it simply, we do not understand ALS, but there is hope. Emerging medicine is paving the way for a better tomorrow. I'm developing a number of strategies to cure ALS, and stem cell therapy is one of them. Today, we have muscle boosters that can stop or slow muscle atrophy. By doing certain exercises, you can prevent muscle pain and spasms. There are even medicines that can boost the immune system to fight neurodegeneration. Lot of drugs are making their way to the clinic.

'I have personally witnessed ALS reversals! Rare events do occur! You are not going to fight the disease alone; we are there for you. My team at Penn will support you at every step along the journey, and they will help you face the challenges of the disease. What you need is a multidisciplinary approach and comprehensive care to fight ALS, and at Penn, you'll get both! I'm sure that one fine day, some brilliant researcher is going to get lucky and find a cure to ALS. That day is just around the corner. So, keep your hopes alive and try to meet me as soon as possible.'

Murali's videoconference with Richard ended on a positive note. Quick decisions were made. Tickets were booked. Visas were stamped. Murali was all set to fly to New York.

***

Richard's discourse made him move with confidence, but the idea of getting himself treated in a foreign city perturbed him. His wife did some advance planning to ensure a pleasant and comfortable journey. The big day arrived and it was tough for Murali to leave Mumbai. His bag was loaded with battery-powered items, medicines, leg braces, vitamin supplements, tissue papers and a BiPAP machine to help him breathe easily at high altitudes. The cab driver came half an hour before time and honked, calling Murali as he peeped out at him from his bedroom window. His wife did some last minute packing and rechecked the flight information.

Before leaving the house, Murali sat down on the sofa in an attitude of desolation, then rose, then sat down again, closed his eyes, and remembered the narrow streets of Kurla, the jostling crowd, the sound of the local train, the festive spirit of the city, the rains, the poor and the deranged, the rich and the powerful, and all and everything about Mumbai. His wife roused him from his reverie and told him to hurry up. It took a lot of time and effort for Murali to get down the stairs. Finally, he managed to get into the cab after nearly 25 minutes of tottering and staggering. The cab started its journey towards Chhatrapati Shivaji

International Airport and Murali's hope for a cure started along with it.

***

It was supposed to be a bit dark outside the airport, but the tall, new air traffic control tower stood like a blazing torch illuminating the scene. Numerous head- and tail-lights injected liveliness into the nightlife of the city. A network of street lights spread across the length and breadth of Mumbai brightened the city, adding to the oft-repeated phrase: Mumbai never sleeps.

There was a sense of excitement in the air as the world was bidding farewell to the old year and gearing up to welcome the new. The year 2016 was just a few hours away and around half of Mumbai's population was welcoming it by dancing and singing under electrifying disco lights in a drunken haze. Migrants desperate to get to their hometowns were clogging the departure points: the airport, railway stations, bus stops and taxi stands. Outside the airport, dazzling fireworks decorated the dark sky with stunning colours. And inside the airport, the overall mood was upbeat.

Chhatrapati Shivaji International Airport was crowded and one could hear the constant chatter of people, the ringing of cell phones and the boarding announcements alerting passengers of the departure of their flights. High-quality duty-free merchandise in charming boutiques lured foreigners by offering great discounts. Many travellers were whiling away their time by catching up with friends on Twitter or Facebook on their laptop computers using free Wi-Fi hotspots. Mobile phones were beeping and vibrating with New Year messages. News footage was running on televisions. One screen showed a graph plotting the behaviour of a chaotic system and the text scrolling across the screen read: *New Chaos Theory to predict unusual extreme events.* Another screen featured a philosopher asking a question, *Do we have free will? Or is it just a big joke?*

Abhishek Patil straightened his tie in the colours of the Indian flag and tied his shoestrings. He was well groomed; his shirt and trousers were clean and pressed to perfection. He walked through the security check-in with a smile on his face and adjusted his overcoat before speaking briefly to one of the air hostesses accompanying him. 'I am going to complete 20,000 flying hours soon,' he remarked. His voice brimmed with arrogance and pride.

Ten minutes later, a high-pitched voice emerged from the flight announcement system. *This is the pre-boarding announcement for flight AI 605 to New York. We are now inviting those passengers with small children, and any passengers requiring special assistance, to begin boarding at this time. Please have your boarding pass and identification ready. Regular boarding will begin in approximately twenty minutes' time. Thank you.*

Boeing 777-300, the metallic marvel, was standing at the gate. Patil spoke to the flight attendant about the weather conditions and ride reports. 'Everything is okay sir, we are good to go,' she said. 'Tell Rakesh to do the walk-around,' said Patil and went to grab a cup of coffee from the terminal before setting up his side of the cockpit.

Rakesh Mehra was the first officer on flight AI 605 and had been Patil's second-in-command for almost two years. He was the flying pilot, though Captain Patil was responsible for the aircraft, its passengers and the crew. Being a long-haul flight, Jatin Doshi had been added to the crew as a relief pilot to assist Rakesh during his rest periods.

As instructed by the captain, Rakesh took a stroll and inspected the overall condition of the aircraft, checking the tire pressure, the status of the oxygen bottles in the cockpit, the wear on the brakes, the engine fan blades for any nicks, and finally eyed the entire airplane for fuel, oil or hydraulic leaks.

Suddenly, a hasty voice emerged from the flight announcement system. *This is the final boarding call for passengers Sudhir Shivaram, Murali Rao, Vandana Rao, Vinod Johri and Ram Johal on flight AI 605 to New York. Please proceed to Gate no. 3 immediately. The final checks are being completed and the captain will order for the doors of the aircraft to close in approximately ten minutes' time. I repeat. This is the final boarding call for Sudhir Shivaram, Murali Rao, Vandana Rao, Vinod Johri and Ram Johal booked on flight AI 605 to New York. Thank you.*

After hearing the announcement, Murali rose slowly and stooped slightly as he walked towards Gate 3. His leg braces gave strength to his weak legs and kept him upright. His wife sighed nervously and looked up into the Mumbai sky through the translucent ceiling, as if she might never see it again.

Meanwhile, in the cockpit, Patil and Rakesh tested their oxygen masks and inspected all the electrical circuit breakers to make sure they were in place. Engine fire detection systems were tested resulting in a bell sound that one might usually hear while boarding the airplane. Rakesh checked everything meticulously: Auxiliary fuel pump – Off, Flight controls – Free and correct, Instruments and Radios – checked and set, Landing gear position lights – Checked, Altimeter – Set, Directional gyro – Set, Fuel gauges – Checked, Trim – Set, Propeller – Exercise, Magnetos – Checked, Engine idle – Checked, Flaps – As required, Seat belts/shoulder harnesses – Fastened, Parking brake – Off, Doors and windows – Locked.

'Sir, we are good to go,' he said to Captain Patil and recited a lengthy, boring pre-flight announcement like a school kid who'd been told to recite multiplication tables. *Ladies and gentleman, welcome onboard Flight AI 605 with non- stop service from Mumbai to New York. We are currently fourth in line for take-off and are expected to be in the air in approximately ten minutes' time. We ask that you fasten your seatbelts at this time and secure all baggage underneath your seat or in the overhead compartments. We also ask that your seats and table trays remain in the upright position for take-off. Please turn off all personal electronic devices, including laptops and cell phones or set your electronic devices to airplane mode until an announcement is made upon arrival. Smoking is not allowed on board, including in the lavatories. Also, use of electronic cigarettes is not allowed. Tampering with, disabling or destroying the smoke detectors in the lavatories is prohibited by law.*

With the help of his wife, Murali settled into his seat on the plane, and listened to the safety instructions as they were read out.

In the event of an emergency, please assume the bracing position. Lean forward with your hands on top of your head and your elbows against your thighs. Ensure your feet are flat on the floor. Should the cabin experience sudden pressure loss, stay calm and listen for instructions from the cabin crew. Oxygen masks will drop down from above your seat. Place the mask over your mouth and nose, like this.

His wife gave him some pills to beat his anxiety.

Pull the strap to tighten it. If you are travelling with children, make sure that your own mask is on first before helping your children. In the unlikely event of an emergency landing and evacuation, leave your carry-on items behind. A life vest is located in a pouch under your seat or between the armrests.

The news feed on his smart phone told Murali that researchers had made an exciting discovery about ALS. A new gene touted to be the cause of ALS had been discovered by a bunch of scientists.

We ask that you make sure that all carry-on luggage is stowed away safely during the flight. While we wait for take-off, please take a moment to review the safety data in the seat pocket in front of you.

The runway was cleared for take-off. Captain Abhishek Patil spoke into the microphone *Flight attendants prepare for take-off please.*

The engine started buzzing; the aircraft began its accelerating run along the runway, and within a few minutes, AI 605 was just a tiny speck in the sky, a blip on the radar. Cruising at an altitude of 20,000 feet, at airspeed of 300 miles per hour, AI 605 was flying above the clouds where the air started to thin and it was also getting smoother. Just then, a voice came cutting through the cabin air trying to get some attention of the passengers on board.

Ladies and gentlemen, the Captain has turned off the Fasten Seat Belt sign, and you may now move around the cabin. However, we always recommend keeping your seat belt fastened while you're seated. You may now turn on your electronic devices such as cell phones, and laptops, but we suggest keeping them on airplane mode.

Murali's wife enquired about the in-flight medical emergency kit.

In a few moments, the flight attendants will be passing around the cabin to offer you hot or cold drinks, as well as a light snack and you can use the monitor in front of you to browse our in-flight entertainment. Now, sit back, relax, and enjoy the flight. Thank you.

The relief pilot, Jatin Doshi, sat near the controls, watching all the glowing buttons and levers in the cockpit. After six hours of smooth flying, fast rivers of air outside shook the plane, causing turbulence strong enough to judder a glass of orange juice kept on the tray table. Captain Patil immediately turned the *seat belt* sign on and spoke briefly: *Cabin crew, please be seated. Ladies and gentleman, we are now crossing a zone of turbulence. Please return to your seats and keep your seat belts fastened. Thank you.*

***

Story 4

Chapter 4: Bombs and Drugs

Some months before the present day

A sequestered small hut faced a barren field, surrounded by thick woods. The harsh August sun roasted the straw and twigs that formed the roof of the hut. Standing at a distance of about 200 steps from the hut, Ram Johal pushed his fingers into the thickness of his unruly hair and scratched his scalp. The unforgiving sun punished him by sapping his spirit and energy. After a bit of heaving and panting, he pitched forward from his position and walked towards the hut with renewed determination.

Inside, the hut smelled of alcohol, and had only two small rooms with many cracks in the walls. The only piece of furniture in the living room was a lumpy bed and sleeping on it was a dhoti-clad shirtless man.

The flimsy front door was closed but the window was ajar. Ram reached the front door of the hut and saw the still shadow of a man through the window. Wasting no time, he wound a rusty cycle chain around his fist and pounded on the door violently. The thumping jolted the shirtless man like a current, waking him from his siesta. Terrified, he armed himself with a knife and shifted his gaze from the front door to a red briefcase. The pounding grew heavier. He tucked the knife in his dhoti and looked around the room. A winnowing basket caught his attention. Without wasting a second, he hid the briefcase under the basket and approached the front door with caution. The pounding stopped. He settled into a fighting stance, holding the knife in his hand. There was tension in the air.

Before he could react, Ram broke open the door of the hut and advanced towards him and punched him in the nose. The knife flew from his hand and landed near the basket. It happened in a jiffy and the power behind the punch was so strong that it took some time for the shirtless man to get up. With his practised boxer's fist, Ram punched him again in his left cheek. Blood spurted from the man's mouth and everything went black before his eyes.

A bottle of arrack changed the course of events. Small, trivial events often lead to catastrophes. According to the plan, the dhoti-clad man was supposed to reach Hotel Victoria, Colaba, at noon with the *maal*. Xavier had told him to stay put in the air-conditioned confines of the hotel room till 6 p.m. and instructed him to venture out after twilight to his secret den – an unmarked house at the end of a quiet road adjacent to the hotel. Instead, he had bought a bottle of arrack, stayed in his hut, and pocketed the money that had been given to him to book a hotel room.

Slowly, very slowly, the man opened his terror-filled eyes and looked at Ram. At first, all he saw were some drifting spiral waves but after a few seconds the waves turned into the outline of a man – not one, but two men.

'Where's the powder? If you give it to me, I'll let you breathe or else you're going to hell!' said Ram, his tone brusque.

Meanwhile, Ali lounged against the wall to see Ram in action. When punches, blows and kicks didn't work, Ram got the truth out of the man at gun point. The red briefcase was out in the open. Ram placed the briefcase on his lap, and unlocked the clasps. After checking the contents, he blurted, 'I think it's a briefcase full of cocaine!'

The contents gave off a stale odour that filled the room. Ali knew what to do. He took a closer look and sniffed some sample packets. 'It's not cocaine; it's a cocaine lookalike. I think you forgot everything I taught you,' he said. Ram cursed himself and tuned his ears to listen to Ali's expert comments.

'While dealing with drugs your nose should take precedence over your eyes. Can't you smell stale urine? It's Mephedrone, also known as meow meow. It's a new entrant on Mumbai's party circuit. A single dose will make you crave sex. When it was legal, nobody bothered about it, but when government banned it, all the drug addicts of Mumbai went crazy! High doses of meow meow will exploit the inner workings of your brain and drive you crazy! It's a hit among the youth!'

'Have you ever had meow meow?' asked Ram.

'Yeah!'

'What's it like?'

'It stings you initially but after some time it reaches your brain and activates the sex neurons. I snorted half a gram and my eyeball almost fell out of its socket! Sometimes it made me go cross-eyed. Even shitty music sounded like Mozart. It softened me and my ego was crushed. It compelled me to do more and every time I redosed it was ecstasy! I was oscillating between dream and reality. If you snort it after sunset, you can't sleep. I was awake all night like an owl, looking at everything without blinking. Once, like a tough guy, I snorted 150mg straight up and I was ready for a fuck. I got an instant erection. Meow meow is like a ticket to enter psychedelic territory. Even dickheads speak philosophy after consuming it.'

'Will this be enough to fulfil our needs?' asked Ram.

'I don't think so…but it's worth a few lakhs…Okay, let's not waste time. Tie him to that pole and put tape on his mouth. Let's get moving!'

Following Ali's instructions, Ram took him up on his shoulders and brought him to the pole. The dhoti-clad man couldn't even move. After tying him up, Ram plastered his mouth and transferred the powder packets from the briefcase to a leather bag.

As they were leaving the hut, Ali heard a vibrating sound. A portion of the room was lit by light coming from a smartphone. It was a phone call from Xavier. If he had called the dhoti-clad man a minute later, the story would have been different. What a coincidence! Two distinct events happened at the same time to give me a story. To the dhoti-clad man it was an untimely coincidence as Xavier was calling to enquire into his whereabouts. Sometimes the law of attraction fails! Things don't happen when you want them to, and vice versa.

Unable to move, the man fixed his gaze on the phone with a frightened look on his face. Ali's eyes went wide and his feet moved swiftly towards the vibrating sound. Then he narrowed his eyes and glanced at the display. It read, "X Calling." *It must be Xavier calling for his meow meow,* he thought. Cautiously, he received the call, his ear glued to the phone. Xavier spoke a few quick words, assuming that he was talking to his partner.

'I'm waiting for you at my place near the hotel. Did you check in? Where's my cat? Also, you'll have to receive the African at the airport tonight. It's very, very important! 11 p.m. sharp! Do you understand?'

There was no answer.

'Are you there? Are you there? Or are you fucking deaf?'

There was no response.

Xavier disconnected and silence engulfed the room for a few seconds. Then, Ali broke the silence by giving instructions to Ram. 'I think the African is carrying some worthy stuff. Hurry up! We can't leave this bloke here … bring him along with us … We have a job to do.'

***

Sweat drenched his white t-shirt and revealed his big arms. Scratching his curl beard, Mbangwa smiled at the customs officer and the officer returned his smile. The catalyst for his smile was the bribe that he had taken from Mbangwa's boss to clear his consignment.

After coming out of the airport, Mbangwa waited near the taxi stand for someone who did not turn up. At the end of his patience, he headed towards his favourite street stall for a smoke. On the table, colourful cigarette packets were arranged in a pyramid. The shopkeeper knew his choice of cigarette and gave him his favourite brand. Constructing another pyramid from a fresh stock of packets, the shopkeeper spoke to Mbangwa in a hushed tone. 'Were you successful in delivering the *maal* last time?'

'Yes,' said Mbangwa and exhaled a series of smoke rings. 'I was expecting someone but he didn't turn up. Could you arrange for a taxi?' he asked the shopkeeper. The shopkeeper took his cell phone out, pressed some buttons, and called his friend.

'I've arranged for a taxi. He'll be coming soon,' he said and Mbangwa thanked him with two bottles of Johnnie Walker, and pressed a bundle of cash in his hand. The shopkeeper took the Johnnie and the cash and slipped it into his drawer.

'Anything you need in Mumbai, Ramlal is at your service,' he grinned.

Ramlal was Mbangwa's sidekick and did some odd jobs for him. He was also well known in police circles and was greeted frequently by the constables and inspectors who flocked to his shop for a free smoke.

Within a few minutes, the taxi had arrived, and the driver, wearing a dirty khaki shirt, greeted Ramlal and told Mbangwa to hop in. 'Take him to Hotel Delmonte,' Ramlal said.

***

The taxi reached a dilapidated hotel on a corner. The board atop the hotel read: HOTEL DELMONTE – *STAY AND HAVE FUN.* Mbangwa walked through a narrow entrance that led him into a spacious lobby with no receptionist at the desk. A young lady sitting in one of the chairs was fixing her makeup.

'Rough night,' she muttered to someone over the phone. Half-listening to her chatter, Mbangwa stole a glance at her. She was attractive and her hair was a shade of brown. Her clothes were cut to exhibit a full figure and the overall ambience of the hotel demonstrated the fact that Delmonte gave *baksheesh* to local cops to overlook what went on inside. Mbangwa waited a while, and after some time, a fat man who knew Ramlal gave him the keys and ushered him into a small room where the room boy was doing some last minute dusting. The walls were dirty and the air smelled of cigarette smoke.

Mbangwa eased into the semi-circular bed that occupied most of the room and turned on the AC. On the wall behind the TV was a sign that read: 'Sex and Drugs and Smoke.' That reminded him of the powder. *It's a tough job*, he chuntered inwardly and glanced around uneasily. To his surprise he began to sweat and walked a few steps to beat his nervousness. After a while he switched the television on.

Acting on a tip-off, Murali Rao and his team busted an inter-state gang of drug peddlers trying to smuggle 34kg of cannabis into the city. All were arrested on the spot.

A week ago, Murali and his team arrested four drug peddlers and seized around 2kg of heroin worth lakhs of rupees.

In another case, Murali Rao and his team laid a trap near Mulund, in which three drug peddlers were arrested. They were found in possession of 100 grams of Amphetamine worth 9 lakh rupees. Murali Rao looked at him through the screen. Little did he know that he would soon see Mbangwa's dead face.

When his nervousness cleared, Mbangwa's anxiety started. He snorted a line of cocaine to beat it and called Xavier from his cell phone.

'I've arrived. Your guy didn't turn up. This is giving me the jitters.'

'I'll explain later. Where's my Big C?'

'It's safe with me. And it is pure – no additives.'

'That's great! I'll come to collect the *maal* myself.'

'No! First you give me half the money and then I deliver the *maal*. You'll check the powder and pay the rest – that's the way it's gonna be.'

'Okay. Give me a day or two to arrange the funds and let's meet at our usual place.'

'Are you nuts? This is not some cheap smack, you asshole! It's worth crores!'

'Okay! Okay! I know a safe place in Kurla.'

'Where in Kurla?'

They were talking about the location and a small audio recorder recorded what Mbangwa said. The room boy who made very little money, and worked very hard, had expertly placed a device under the semi-circular bed. Ram had given him three thousand rupees and it was too much money to refuse. It all started with Xavier spilling the beans on the African over the phone. Ali did his part by getting the passengers' manifest and Ram spied on Mbangwa like a hawk. After getting the recorder from the room boy, Ram connected it to a laptop and heard Mbangwa's conversation with Xavier. Then he called Ali and spoke to him in an enthusiastic tone.

'I've got good news for you.'

***

'Stop beating him, we got what we wanted!' said Ali to one of his henchmen.

There was dried blood on his dhoti and he had a swollen cheek. Ali instructed his men to lock the man up in a room. The dhoti-clad man stayed loyal to Xavier till the end and had refused to divulge anything to Ali's men, even at the risk of death. But his disappearance had alerted Xavier.

Meanwhile, Ram met Ali at his place and told him about the Big C. Ali devised a new plan; his team would snatch Xavier's *maal* from the African and chose Ram to be their front-runner. Ali spoke about installing his men as a back-up to help Ram if things go haywire.

None of them knew that a nasty surprise awaited them. Xavier phoned Mbangwa the day before the D-Day from a public booth and shocked him with his words. He put his criminal mind to use and devised a counterattack to teach a harsh lesson to his enemies. 'We won't go ahead with the plan. Let's choose another day,' he said and that changed the course of events. Another twist in the story. Another change which would give birth to many more changes in the future.

'Why the sudden change of plan?' Mbangwa asked.

'I think somebody is snooping on us. The guy who was supposed to pick you up from the airport vanished without a trace. Where's the *maal*? Safe?'

'Yes! In that case, give me a date quickly, I want to close this deal as soon as possible,' said Mbangwa, and wiped the sweat off his face.

'Sure! But let's catch the mouse first!' said Xavier and told one of his henchmen to act like an informer. Following his instructions, the henchman called the ANC headquarters from a PCO and tipped them off on the deal. The original plan had been that Xavier would execute the deal near Kurla but now that he suspected someone of tracking his moves, he laid a trap to catch the mouse by making an anonymous tip-off to the police. Even Ali exercised caution while allocating his men for D-Day. Time moved swiftly and D-Day arrived.

***

The insects were roused to action by the full moon. Old cars stripped down and reduced to their parts were piled on both sides of the road, forming a heap of scrap. Adjacent to the lonely road was a big scrapyard surrounded by thick vegetation. One could enter the yard through its front gate or by walking through the vegetation. The circular yard had junk piled up on its circumference and hiding behind the junk was one of Murali's men in plain clothes. Another police officer dressed like a rag-picker was hiding near the front gate. Thick vegetation close to the scrapyard served as a good hiding place for Ali's men. A stray dog with a torn ear was standing at the centre of the scrapyard where the deal was expected to happen. Minutes turned to hours and Murali shook his head in disgust on seeing his watch. It was late, past 11:30, and the Nigerian had been supposed to come with the *maal* at 11:00. Waiting in anticipation, Murali took a cigarette, put it to his lips and activated his walkie-talkie.

'Any update? Did you guys see anyone?'

'I've been waiting here for two hours! No sign of anyone, sir,' one of the men replied.

'Okay. Keep moving and tell me if you see anyone suspicious,' said Murali.

After a few minutes, more dogs entered the scrapyard for a midnight communion. They were barking for no reason. Ram was hiding in the bushes. His forehead was sticky with sweat. Just then a faint noise emanated from the bushes. Ram turned to look, and saw two figures ducking and inching towards the yard. The voice in his head started its monologue: *Are they cops? Xavier's men? What are they doing here? I guess they didn't see me. It's going to be twelve o'clock ... still no sign of the African. Let me wait and watch.*

Everyone was anxiously waiting for the African to arrive. Some rustling sounds were heard but it was the breeze swirling a few dry leaves. After some barking and yelping, the dogs left the scrapyard but Ali's men were waiting like hungry dogs to snatch Xavier's *maal* from the African. They waited unwearyingly till dawn before realizing that Xavier had played a trick and fooled them all. Luckily, Murali's team did not spot them and Ram decided to follow the wait-and-strike strategy.

***

It was a lazy Sunday afternoon and Ali was in the mood for a hit. He was sitting on a mat with his legs spread wide as if he were ready for a fuck. Wearing nothing but boxer shorts, he was taking it easy at his place. Ram Johal was there too, his face etched with ebullience. With his hands in his pockets, he asked Ali to guess the contents. Maintaining his lazy posture, Ali enquired about the contents and Ram's reply made him sit upright, his cheeks flushed with excitement.

'I've got *Charas* from Himachal, Ali *bhai*! Quality stuff. You should try some.'

Ram took out two green balls sealed in a small plastic cover and tore one of them to make a joint. Ali pulled out two Gold Flake Kings, while Ram, with steady hands, concentrated on the task of making tiny *Charas* balls. With his head tilted back, Ali toasted the cigarette with a lighter for a few seconds.

'Ram, we have to be on our toes this time. When is he making the next attempt to deliver the *maal*?'

'Soon, very soon, Ali *bhai*. I'll let you know once I get the information.'

'This time we will have to sneak in like wolves and snatch the *maal* from the Nigerian before Xavier gets it. I'm still wondering why he failed to arrive at the scene. I think Xavier is trying to play games with me. Good that you were not spotted by anyone. '

Ram took the cigarette, made a thin line with his tongue, and ripped it along the line to get the tobacco out. Then he mixed the *Charas* with the tobacco, and made two spliffs, one for him and one for Ali. They both took a deep drag of *Charas* and their tough lungs absorbed all the dirty ingredients. Soon, the room was filled with serious conversation and smoke.

'It took me many years to build this empire and become a kingpin. If Xavier gets the *maal* he can topple everything that

I built over all these years. I won't let anyone set foot in my territory,' said Ali and savoured the high of his joint.

Ram knew the deal was important as it involved lots of money. 'We'll get the *maal*, Ali *bhai*, we'll definitely get it.'

'This deal is important as it involves a sizable quantity of cocaine. If Xavier gets the *maal*, he'll rule the market, but if we get it, we'll rule the market. But ultimately, it's not about money or cocaine. You know it and I know it. Yes, money is important, but I'm going to use it as a tool to achieve my motive. I'm not like Xavier, spending money on swanky cars and luxurious apartments. I'm not a cheap drug dealer. As a matter of fact, I'm a jihadi! We are jihadis! We live and die for our motive, not money. I need someone with a good appetite for risk and who is bold. And that's why I chose you for my mission.

'The world has changed, people have become cosmopolitans, but they still carry their religion in their hearts and view others through the fabric of religion. So, you not being a Muslim is an added advantage for me. And there are other reasons for selecting you. Your name is one of the reasons – Ram. With a godly, Hindu name like that, you'll have no problems with American security at the airport. The thing to remember is, once you do this job for me, your family will be my family. I'll take care of your ailing mother. I'll find a bridegroom for your sister and get her married. I'm not merely enacting a scene from a Bollywood movie; I'm telling the truth! You have to believe me.'

They inhaled more *Charas* and filled their nostrils with smoke. It took some time for Ali to explain to Ram his strategy. The plan was told to him in detail, with long pauses until all the joints had melted into roaches.

***

Salim put on his low-waist jeans and T-shirt; his pot belly stretched the imprint on his T-shirt that read "Sex & the City." He took a local train to Mulund, his destination a massage parlour that hid amidst the cluster of small houses at the end of a deserted road. He picked his way through the streets and reached the front door. He knocked on the translucent glass and waited for Pinky to show up but there was no response. After waiting for a few minutes, he pushed the door open and entered the public area of the parlour that housed two sofas and a counter. A bevy of women in tight clothes were sipping tea. A lady pimp was sitting at the counter, reading a Hindi magazine. A cross-eyed tea vendor poured some tea into a styrofoam cup and served it to the lady. Salim tapped on the counter to get her attention. She looked up from her magazine with a grin. 'Hi Salim *ji*! What can I do for you?'

'Where's Pinky? Boss wants her at his place,' said Salim. The very next second he was distracted by the smells coming from a display of cheap perfumes.

'Are you in a hurry? How about some tea?' the lady asked.

'I'm not in a mood to hear your prattle. Where's Pinky?'

She got up with a sigh and Salim followed her down the corridor that led to the private area. There was a small room with an attached bathroom to his right. The pimp switched on the lights, and the room filled with a soft yellowish glow. A massage table, which looked like a soft bed, was decorated with rose petals in the shape of a heart. Everything was bathed in white except for the mauve, sperm-stained sheets – a memento of all the excited customers who had come in to get a happy ending or a blow job. Fluffy pillows were positioned to help customers get maximum results during their body-to-body massage sessions. A shelf next to the bed displayed an assortment of oils and lotions and some tissue papers to wipe off sperm after a hand job.

'Pinky! Pinky! Come out … Salim wants you.'

Pinky came out of the bathroom and smiled at Salim. She was a sexy, thirtyish female escort with long black hair plaited like a South Indian bride; the braid rested between her breasts and its placement pulled Salim's eyes. Her figure was sculpted to perfection.

Salim got straight to the point. 'Listen … Boss wants you at his place for a session.'

'Let's go!' Pinky said immediately.

'He wants you to be decked up in this red saree,' said Salim and gave her a bright red saree.

Without saying another word, she got dressed and they left for Xavier's private bungalow. Xavier came hurrying from his bedroom. He gestured Pinky toward the stairs leading to their private den and she obeyed him instantly. Salim was ready to take further instructions and Xavier told him to get a new SIM card. After inserting the card in his smart phone he called Mbangwa whilst turning his back on Salim. He told Mbangwa to listen carefully and spoke softly but Salim was able to hear every word.

'There's an abandoned temple near Rutu Park in Thane – close to the lake – that's where we'll meet.'

'What time?' asked Mbangwa.

'12:45 sharp!' said Xavier and turned towards Salim without any warning. He spotted Salim in a thinking posture.

'Why are you still here? asked Xavier.

Salim stood frozen to his spot and he couldn't reply immediately.

'You don't seem to be your normal self. What's the matter?'

Salim reacted to his question with a broad smile and behaved as if everything's normal. Xavier commanded him to leave the room at once.

***

Khabree stepped out of the VT station and entered a country liquor shop. He was wearing a T-shirt with a message GAME OVER and matching corduroy pants with many pockets. Passing a mirror, he glanced into it and surveyed his features.

Sleepless nights had given him dark circles around his eyes. He knew that anything could happen to him at any time. There was a lot of risk in his line of work, being a stool pigeon and giving information about crooks to the police. He worked for Murali and other police officers, and had established his position as a trusted informer.

Today he felt sick and nervous and his inner voice went on and on like a woodpecker's peck. To beat his anxiety he prepared a shot of whiskey and gulped it down, then licked some pickles to get a high. He was nervous about the message he had to deliver. It was not an ordinary news about cheap thieves. The tip was worth a lot of money. Not merely tens of thousands – his standard fee for one authentic tip; it was worth hundreds of thousands or even more. He thought about cocaine worth crores and gulped another shot to get some courage.

After finishing his quota of drinks he decided to go home. Outside, the scene was misty and dim. Suddenly he felt unsafe. The weight of the news almost crushed him. Ask a khabree and he'll tell you that all events in this world are not pre-determined. People in his world can act unreasonably and can choose to do anything. For him, human freedom is not an illusion but a reality. His world works on the concept of free will. He can be killed on sight or be spared. He felt like getting slaughtered when the local train to Thane jerked to life and moved out of VT station.

Khabree's hut in Thane had one room equipped with the latest gadgets. He lived with his mother, brother and sister. His real name was Prakash but friends in his circle knew him as *Khabree*. He carried a total of eight smart phones, all of them given by police officers. After taking charge as ACP, Murali had fuelled the idea of government jobs for khabrees to provide them a steady stream of income but the implementation of his programme had failed miserably. Then he launched a secret fund to pay khabrees and gifted a touch phone to Prakash for his service.

Prakash entered his hut, sat on the floor, leaned his back against the wall and assumed a relaxed position. After taking a deep breath he dug into his pocket and pulled out Murali's phone. Then he inserted a new SIM and after that he was distracted, for a while, by Salim's words. 'If things go right you'll put some money in my pocket.'

Salim and Prakash had been best buddies since they had been at government school together. Salim's parents were part of the flesh trade and ran a massage parlour providing extra services. Life didn't go their way as police raided their parlour and put them in jail when they refused to pay monthly *hafta* to the area inspector. Salim never saw them again. Inspired by his parents' legacy, he had worked as a pimp before getting into drugs. Xavier had employed him to be his assistant and taught him to sell drugs. It had taken him seven years to get promoted to being Xavier's trusted aide.

Prakash was at the other end of the spectrum, working hard, while Salim got easy money. Before becoming a police informer Prakash had done some menial jobs to support his family. He often complained about his bad financial situation to Salim. As a mark of friendship, Salim decided to help him, and spilled the beans on the cocaine deal.

'Prakash, listen to me, I have a gold mine for you. A drug mule is here in Mumbai with 25 crores worth of powder. Pure cocaine! He's going to sell it to my boss. There's an abandoned temple near Rutu Park in Thane – close to the lake – that's where the deal is going to happen. Your countdown starts now. Exactly 62 hours to go! It's going to be real quick and everything will get over in 10 minutes. Ask for a 10% cut from the cops and if things go right you'll put some money in my pocket. And don't worry about me – I'll never be suspected and I know how to handle Xavier.'

After inserting the SIM, Prakash called Murali to discuss money. 'The mule is still roaming with the *maal*. Cocaine worth 25 crores has still not reached its owner. I'll give you the information but you'll have to agree to my terms and conditions. I need a 10% cut if things go according to the plan.'

'10% is too high! Okay! I agree. Place? Time?'

'There's an abandoned temple near Rutu Park in Thane – close to the lake – that's where the deal is going to happen.

Sharp at 00:45 hours and I want 10% cut if you guys catch them red-handed.'

***

Animals don't perceive time as we do, and their actions are mechanical. They are born with a preloaded program which provokes the same reaction every single time even when presented with a different stimulus – but we human beings are a bit different. Our genetic makeup is complex and our actions are unpredictable. A small change in brain chemistry is all that it takes to turn a sane person into a schizophrenic and a handful of them can teach us what we do not know about uncertainty. Things took a new turn when Xavier decided to change his plan again.

The goldfish jerked back to life and reacted favourably by swimming rapidly around the fish tank. It was breakfast time and they mouthed for food after seeing Xavier. He fed the goldfish and sat in the arm chair by the window. It was an important day and he had woken to it like a schoolboy before an examination. About 17 miles from his place, in a closed room, Mbangwa was feverishly stacking cocaine packets into two big bags. Not far from his building, there was a small shop selling beedis and cigarettes. One of Ali's men, who had been told to keep an eye on the mule, was smoking a beedi, waiting for him to exit. His hopeful eyes saw two thugs entering the building.

Xavier was preparing for a battle and something inside him told that tonight is going to be tough. Many racing thoughts stunned him for a while and after doing some mental calculations he nodded his head. 'Yes, that's the way to go,' he said to himself, and dug out his phone to call Mbangwa.

'What's the matter?' Mbangwa sounded nervous.

'There's a change in the plan.'

'I guess something has gone off inside your head. Are you nuts?'

'We'll meet at 8 tonight, not 00:45,' said Xavier.

'Do you foresee any danger?'

'Keep your cool! This is just a precaution. Any information that remains unchanged for a considerable time can be compromised,' said Xavier and ended the call.

Just then the doorbell rang. Mbangwa opened the door and welcomed the thugs. One was a fat man with pockmarks on his face and the second had the build of a bull. After filling the bags with cocaine, Mbangwa armed himself with a pistol and a torch.

Time passed swiftly. Mbangwa and his bodyguards walked out of the building. Ali's sidekick who was eating sukha bhel from a paper cone saw them coming out of the front gate. A car came to a screeching halt in front of them. Mbangwa took the front seat and the bodyguards took the back, guarding the cocaine bags. The car started its journey towards Thane and Ali's sidekick followed them on his bike. Ram was taken aback when Ali's sidekick told him about Mbangwa's early start.

'That's surprising! Xavier likes to conduct his business at late hours. Follow him carefully. Don't lose sight of him. Switch on your GPS. I'll be there,' said Ram.

***

It was a moonless night and the sky was empty with no stars to fill the dark firmament. The road beside the lake was deserted. Street lights that ran across the deserted road, planted at regular intervals, were poorly lit. A line of tall trees on both sides of the lane added to the poor visibility. A dilapidated building stood near the lake, touching the deserted road. Next to it stood an abandoned temple. Everything was bathed in a dull yellow.

Mbangwa's car entered the deserted road. The lane was silent except for the shrieking noise from the engine. Irritated by the sound, Mbangwa told the driver to stop the car and gave him a 1000-rupee note, telling him to scoot. Sitting inside the car, he booted his laptop. An instant later he plugged the data card to access the Internet. He sifted through his online bank page to see if Xavier had transferred half the money as promised. Bingo! Xavier had kept his word. Wasting no time he took out the car keys, gave them to one of the thugs and said, 'Hit the main road and wait for us.' The other thug slung the bags over his shoulders and followed Mbangwa. They walked cautiously towards the threshold of the temple.

Ram tracked his partner with the help of the GPS and joined him at the beginning of the deserted road. They moved in a quiet, stealthy way and found a good hiding place behind the dilapidated building. 'From here we can see the threshold of the temple,' said Ram. At 19:55 by the digital clock on Ram's mobile phone, a car entered the deserted road.

'Put the car into first gear and drive slowly till you reach the temple,' said Xavier and felt the pistol in his jeans pocket. He was carrying a 9mm semiautomatic handgun with a built-in silencer. The engine stuttered to a halt near the building and two men got out of the car. Xavier's sidekick was carrying a sports bag big enough to accommodate a 17-year-old boy.

When Xavier reached the threshold of the temple he saw Mbangwa, standing with his partner.

'Where's the *maal*?' asked Xavier, and Mbangwa's partner revealed the bags.

Xavier was relieved. 'That's good! Hope you got the money. I want you to throw me some samples. I want to do a taste test.'

'I've not come all the way from Africa to sell you baking powder or some bullshit. It's pure! Trust me! No cutting agents!' said Mbangwa. But Xavier insisted on testing the samples and Mbangwa gestured to his partner to appease him.

Meanwhile, Ram's partner moved like a cat and took a new position to do some surveillance from a different angle. Xavier took a pinch of coke and put it on his tongue to check the purity. The *maal* numbed him at once. 'Seems to be of good quality … ' he thought. He experienced similar sensation when he rubbed some coke on his gums.

Things just seemed to go his way, but Ram's aim disrupted his plan, and altered the course of the story. To everyone's surprise, Mbangwa's partner suddenly dropped the cocaine bags. It took them a few seconds to realize that he had been shot.

***

'Will Ram succeed?' Ali questioned himself. He drowned his tension by gulping three shots of vodka and stared at the TV to divert his mind. His eyes settled on a BBC report, where a blonde reporter spoke about Islamic terror attacks in America.

The new millennium began with a bang for the United States. Two suicide bombers from al-Qaeda sailed on a fiberglass boat carrying explosives and bombed a US warship. The explosion shocked the country and ripped a hole in the hull of the ship, killing 17 US sailors who were lining up for lunch. Around 200 to 300 kgs of explosives were used and it created a 40-by-60-foot gash in the ship's port side. Osama bin Laden celebrated the attack and warned of similar attacks in the future.

The September 11 attacks were discussed and planned at the Kuala Lumpur al-Qaeda summit. The idea of crashing planes into buildings were dreamed up in a posh hotel room in Malaysia. The World Trade Center collapsed. Some 2750 people were killed in New York, 184 at the Pentagon, and 40 in Pennsylvania. The attacks blew people into pieces and even the most advanced DNA techniques couldn't identify victims. This was the second terrorist attack on the World Trade Center, the first one being carried out by a group of Muslim terrorists in 1993. Then, a 590 kg bomb made of urea nitrate and other booster explosives was loaded on a truck and was detonated below the North Tower. The idea was to topple the North Tower crashing into the South Tower, but the attack was foiled.

Next attack came from a Muslim American who shouted "Allahu Akbar" before gunning down 13 American soldiers and wounding over 30 others in a mass shootout on an American military base. The incident lasted for 10 minutes and the shooter was considered a hero by Islamic extremists. According to the testimony from witnesses, the shooter spared the civilians and targeted soldiers in uniform. On that day, Fort Hood was full of blood and bullets. A total of 214 rounds were fired; 146 spent shell casings were recovered inside the building and 68 casings were collected outside.

On Patriots' Day, marathon runners ran for their lives when two pressure cooker bombs exploded near the marathon's finish line on Boylston Street. Two young lads with extremist Islamic beliefs filled their backpacks with pressure-cooker bombs packed with shrapnel and other materials and placed them on the ground amidst marathon enthusiasts. The blast killed 3 spectators and injured more than 260 people.

The common adage is that it is the duty of all Muslims to kill Americans. It is a religious war! A war of ideologies! Anti-American feeling among Muslims is on the rise, and they deeply resent the West.

We talk about universal brotherhood. We talk about joining hands together against injustice. We talk about one caste, one religion and one god for everyone. We talk about love. We talk about bliss. We talk about beatitude. We read lengthy commentaries about peace but we are all the time preparing for a war! We do not know when the next attack will come … We all are marching towards disaster!'

Ali replied to her speech and said, 'The next attack will come from us and it will come soon! Truck bombs and pressure cooker bombs are passé – we are coming up with new flavours! Radioactive bombs! Dirty bombs!'

*****

The gunshot sound was not that loud – partly because of the silencer and partly because of the loud chirping of crickets. The bullet stung his abdomen and he wobbled, dropping to his knees. Seeing the man's posture, Mbangwa exercised caution and hid behind the temple wall. Xavier and his partner reacted to the situation and ducked behind a pile of junk near the temple. The cocaine bags were lying on the ground, unattended. Mbangwa's boy crawled into the bushes to save himself from being shot again; he tried to stand up but pain dragged him down. With trembling arms, he crawled through the wilderness of weeds and bushes and on his way encountered Ram's partner. They fought. Punching sounds were heard followed by rustling in the bushes. After some time, abruptly, all sounds ceased and others stood listening to the silence.

Ram made the first move. With the confidence of a marksman he advanced towards the cocaine bags. His first bullet had caught the target's abdomen and he was left with five shots in his gun.

Xavier cocked his handgun and peeped from his hiding place to assess the situation. A few shots were exchanged between Ram and Xavier, the gunshots sounding like someone spitting saliva. Mbangwa was waiting for Ram's head to surface and fired two shots to prove his existence. Both bullets missed Ram by a couple of inches. When Xavier's boy moved again, he got shot in his leg. Ram's bullet pierced his knee and he limped towards the car to save himself from getting shot again.

The shooting continued. Mbangwa decided to risk everything and made two little hops to get a clear view of the cocaine bags. Ram was left with only one shot and to his surprise the bullet found its mark. When Peter got into the taxi and said, 'Take me to Thane,' Ram felt his index finger on the curve of the trigger. And when the taxi engine sputtered to life, Ram pressed the trigger.

We are creatures of planning. We plan our future and always expect things to happen according to our design, but we fail to understand that a stranger can change the course of our lives. The bullet left the gun, but the little noise that it made was once again subdued by the chirping of crickets. Mbangwa had to accept the inevitable – a gunshot wound to his liver. 'Fuck!' he shouted in pain and fell to the ground. One eye went blurry and he was slowly losing consciousness.

The cocaine bags lay equidistant from Ram and Xavier. The guns fell silent and all the bullets were exhausted. With no other options left, both Ram and Xavier readied themselves for a fist fight.

When they clashed, it was evident that Ram was stronger than Xavier. Mbangwa watched the fighting helplessly. Blood gushed from Xavier's nose and spread over his lips. He spat blood and skipped forward to attack Ram. But instead he got punched in the face. Xavier clenched his teeth, flung his hands in the air and shook his head to show Ram that he was piqued by his nasty blows.

'You still want to fight?' asked Ram.

Xavier threw himself at Ram in a fit of rage, but ended up getting jabbed again.

'Do you want a fucking knockout punch?' asked Ram.

Xavier studied Ram's face. He could already picture himself getting beaten to death. Instead of fighting Ram, he reached for the bags, but got kicked. The fist fight turned hazy in Mbangwa's eyes and after some time everything went black. When he opened his eyes again, he saw Xavier running for his life. Silence conquered everything again and Mbangwa was lying flat on his back with nothing to do but wait for death to come.

***

Two black bags, which looked bulged and overstuffed like the belly of an obese man, were placed in front of Ali for him to examine the contents.

'Fucking bastards, they scurried for cover like frightened chickens and ran for their lives before I could kill them,' said Ram.

Ali laughed, took a sip of his beer, and opened one bag. A feeling of exhilaration swept through him when he saw the cocaine.

'It's pure white money, Ali *bhai*! Worth 25 Crores! But I spilled some powder during my clash with the African.'

'That's okay,' said Ali, and took a packet from the bag. 'Let me check its purity.'

'I rubbed some coke on my gums to check its purity. I think it's authentic!' said Ram.

Ali reacted to his words with a smile and said, 'Even cutting agents will numb your jaw and they are added to mimic the effects of pure cocaine. The heating test is the best method.'

With steady hands, he took a pinch of cocaine and placed it on the heating equipment. It melted at 98°C – a sign that it was pure *maal*! Then he decided to do the ultimate test of snorting the coke to see if it was free from cutting agents. He emptied the powder onto a glass table and made two lines, one for him and one for Ram. He kept his half-finished beer bottle on the floor and readied himself for some snorting. With a rolled 100-rupee note he chased the line and sat back in the corner, letting the drug take hold.

'That's worth the effort, Ram! The *maal* seems to be of good quality! Bravo!' he couldn't contain his excitement.

Ram punched the air in triumph and chased his line. After the effects of cocaine wore off, they got into some serious conversation about their next plan.

'We need to add shit to this *maal* and make money. You guys have to work hard in the streets to make it happen. Once we get the cash in hand, we rule the market. It's important that we convert the money into something legitimate. Like some kind of an investment or a bank account. Then, we'll transfer the money to our gang in a roundabout way. We make the money hop from one account to the other until it reaches the intended recipient, or we do it through the hawala system. Doing things in a circuitous way will keep the sniffers at bay. At the dawn of the New Year, you'll be in New York to execute our plan. Ram, you are our torchbearer! Rafiq will receive you at the airport. He's our bomb expert. He knows how to build a dirty bomb and he will give you a crash course in how to detonate it. You'll have to plant and trigger some dirty bombs in New York.'

'What is a dirty bomb? Is it some kind of a nuclear bomb?' asked Ram.

'Are you kidding? We don't have enough money to deal in nuclear weapons. If nuclear bombs are Tibetan Mastiffs then dirty bombs are nothing but Chihuahuas. They are ordinary bombs mixed with radioactive waste that scatters when the bomb explodes, and that makes it potent, hence the name. They are not built to cause mayhem but there will be unrest. Those near the bomb will be blown to pieces but it's not as destructive as a nuclear bomb.

'Well, the point here is that when the bombs explode, people die! Survivors, relatives, government and other people mourn, and after a couple of days the incident is forgotten.

But when you build a device that is designed to disperse radioactive material over a large area and announce that its contents are highly toxic, then everyone will remember the blast for the rest of their lives. It's not death that freaks people out; it's the fear of death. Our motive is to cause panic, anxiety and fear. We are not dealing with something physical, but psychological. 'You'll go with Rafiq to his secret den where he constructs dirty bombs and learn how to handle them. Preparing them is no big deal but sourcing and handling radioactive materials is. We are taking baby steps towards nuclear terrorism.'

After hearing Ali's commentary on bombs, Ram scratched his head for a while as if nothing had entered his brain but he surprised Ali by asking an intelligent question. 'Has a dirty bomb even been detonated? I mean, I have never heard of such a thing! I don't even remember reading about it in the newspapers.'

The question surprised Ali and he paused to gather his thoughts before answering. 'No. You'll be the first to detonate a dirty bomb if everything goes according to our plan.'

***

Cocaine fever was everywhere and it had spread its wings to other cities in India like Chennai, Hyderabad, Bengaluru, Pune and Indore. Ali had installed his agents in all these cities to make quick money. He moved some of the drugs to other cities via small container ships, pleasure boats, sail boats and fishing boats. Everything went according to plan and the *maal* set his cash registers ringing. He threw some money at technology and sold some of his drugs anonymously over the Internet. He used intelligent programs that changed his IP address, making it difficult for anyone to trace him. He also used secure payment systems and his transactions were encrypted. Selling drugs on the Internet is a double-edged sword but Ali weighed the risks and benefits and operated with caution. He knew a lot of trusted VPN (Virtual Private Network) providers offering true privacy on the Web, unlike fake ones who sold information to others for money. He familiarized himself with cryptocurrencies and the latest encryption technologies. He stayed away from VPN service providers who logged sensitive identifiable information on their servers. By the time Christmas had come, he had sold all the cocaine packets. Funds were distributed to all the stakeholders to make his plan a reality.

New Year was approaching, and Ram's job was to cause mayhem. He said goodbye to his friends and bade a teary farewell to his family. 'Ali *Bhai* will take care of you,' he said. Then he packed his bags and left his place, whistling a sad song.

The road leading to the airport was heavy with traffic and Ali gave some words of wisdom to Ram. 'Collecting radioactive materials is like birds collecting straws to build a nest. It is a tedious task! Rafiq had to bribe officials working in research firms and hospitals to source caesium, cobalt, plutonium and other radioactive materials. Nowadays you can get these things online! The Internet has everything you're looking for. Nobody knows if you are a man or a dog on the Internet!'

The car reached **Chhatrapati Shivaji International Airport**. 'All the best! We'll ride on your skills and courage. Never give up. The police will try to sniff you out but you should stay out of their reach. Our plans are not yesterday's plans; it was conceived a year back and now it is in your hands to make it a reality. We kill Americans and they kill us. When the killers kill, nobody cares about the dead people, but they pop an eye to see the names of the killers and the religion behind their names. That's why I chose you! They can't reach us through you. You are an outlier. You are a Hindu,' said Ali.

His words of encouragement sounded like farewell to Ram. 'All the best! I'm sure that you'll be successful in your mission. And don't worry about your mother and sister, I'll take good care of them. Give me a call once you reach New York.'

Ram nodded and without saying a word, he hugged Ali and mingled with the crowd of passengers.

***

It was supposed to be a bit dark outside the airport, but the tall, new air traffic control tower stood like a blazing torch illuminating the scene. Numerous head- and tail-lights injected liveliness into the nightlife of the city. A network of street lights spread across the length and breadth of Mumbai brightened it, adding to the oft-repeated phrase: Mumbai never sleeps.

There was a sense of excitement in the air as the world was bidding farewell to the old year and gearing up to welcome the new. The year 2016 was just a few hours away and around half of Mumbai's population was welcoming it in a drunken haze by dancing and singing under electrifying disco lights. Migrants desperate to get to their hometowns were clogging the departure points: the airport, railway stations, bus stops, and taxi stands. Outside the airport, dazzling fireworks decorated the dark sky with stunning colours. And inside the airport, the overall mood was upbeat.

Chhatrapati Shivaji International Airport was crowded and one could hear the constant chatter of people, the ringing of cell phones and the boarding announcements alerting passengers of the departure of their flights. High-quality duty-free merchandise in charming boutiques lured foreigners by offering great discounts. Many travellers were whiling away their time by catching up with friends on Twitter or Facebook on their laptop computers using free Wi-Fi hotspots. Mobile phones were beeping and vibrating with New Year messages. News footage was running on televisions. One screen showed a reporter talking about Randomness. *Karma sticks its head out and says if you do good things, you are assured of future happiness and if you do bad things, you are doomed! It thrives on cause- and-effect relationship and it makes definitive statements about future. And it even goes one step further and talks about reincarnation. Fate, determinism, karma and reincarnation, they all have a definitive idea about future, but in reality the world is ruled by randomness and chaos.*

Abhishek Patil straightened his tie in the colours of the Indian flag and tied his shoestrings. He was well groomed; his shirt and trousers were clean and pressed to perfection. His attire was in accordance with the grooming policies of Air India for pilots and his face was etched with a pilot's wisdom. He walked through the security check-in with a smile on his face and adjusted his overcoat before speaking briefly to one of the air hostesses accompanying him. 'I am going to complete 20,000 flying hours soon,' he remarked. His voice brimmed with arrogance and pride.

Ten minutes later, a high-pitched voice emerged from the flight announcement system. *This is the pre-boarding announcement for flight AI 605 to New York. We are now inviting those passengers with small children, and any passengers requiring special assistance, to begin boarding at this time. Please have your boarding pass and identification ready. Regular boarding will begin in approximately twenty minutes' time. Thank you.*

Boeing 777-300, the metallic marvel, was standing at the gate. Patil spoke to the flight attendant about the weather conditions and ride reports. 'Everything is okay sir, we are good to go,' she said. 'Tell Rakesh to do the walk-around,' said Patil and went to grab a cup of coffee from the terminal before setting up his side of the cockpit.

Rakesh Mehra was the first officer on flight AI 605 and had been Patil's second-in-command for almost two years. He was the flying pilot, though Captain Patil was responsible for the aircraft, its passengers, and the crew. Being a long-haul flight, Jatin Doshi had been added to the crew as a relief pilot to assist Rakesh during his rest periods.

As instructed by the captain, Rakesh took a stroll and inspected the overall condition of the aircraft, checking the tire pressure, the status of the oxygen bottles in the cockpit, the wear on the brakes, the engine fan blades for any nicks and finally eyed the entire airplane for fuel, oil or hydraulic leaks.

Suddenly, a hasty voice emerged from the flight announcement system. *This is the final boarding call for passengers Sudhir Shivaram, Murali Rao, Vandana Rao, Vinod Johri and Ram Johal on flight AI 605 to New York. Please proceed to Gate no. 3 immediately. The final checks are being completed and the captain will order for the doors of the aircraft to close in approximately ten minutes' time. I repeat. This is the final boarding call for Sudhir Shivaram, Murali Rao, Vandana Rao, Vinod Johri and Ram Johal booked on flight AI 605 to New York. Thank you.*

Meanwhile, in the cockpit, Patil and Rakesh tested their oxygen masks and inspected all the electrical circuit breakers to make sure they were in place. Engine fire detection systems were tested resulting in a bell sound that one might usually hear while boarding the airplane. Rakesh checked everything meticulously: Auxiliary fuel pump – Off, Flight controls – Free and correct, Instruments and Radios – checked and set, Landing gear position lights – Checked, Altimeter – Set, Directional gyro – Set, Fuel gauges – Checked, Trim – Set, Propeller – Exercise, Magnetos – Checked, Engine idle – Checked, Flaps – As required, Seat belts/shoulder harnesses – Fastened, Parking brake – Off, Doors and windows – Locked.

'Sir, we are good to go,' he said to Captain Patil and recited a lengthy, boring pre-flight announcement like a school kid who'd been told to recite multiplication tables. *Ladies and gentleman, welcome onboard Flight AI 605 with non- stop service from Mumbai to New York. We are currently fourth in line for take-off and are expected to be in the air in approximately ten minutes' time. We ask that you fasten your seatbelts at this time and secure all baggage underneath your seat or in the overhead compartments. We also ask that your seats and table trays remain in the upright position for take-off. Please turn off all personal electronic devices, including laptops and cell phones or set your electronic devices to airplane mode until an announcement is made upon arrival. Smoking is not allowed on board, including in the lavatories. Also, use of electronic cigarettes is not allowed. Tampering with, disabling or destroying the smoke detectors in the lavatories is prohibited by law.*

Ladies and gentlemen, on behalf of the crew I ask that you please direct your attention to the monitors above as we review the emergency procedures. There are six emergency exits on this aircraft. Take a minute to locate the exit closest to you. Note that the nearest exit may be behind you. Count the number of rows to this exit.

As the crew began their take-off rituals, Ram remembered his ailing mother and his unmarried sister. Events from the past flashed before his eyes. His father had been killed for being honest and his memory of the fateful night when the police barged into his chawl to gun him down still plagued him. He had been six years old when he watched the bullet pierce his father's heart through his uniform. His father knew some dark secrets about a politician and had not been willing to hide the truth for a sum of money, no matter how large. The politician had had to kill him.

To support his mother and sister, Ram began his career by stealing petty things, and as time went by, he ventured into drugs and committed violent crimes. His career included a stint as a pimp. That was when he had an altercation with a local don who held a gun to his head and threatened to kill him. Luckily, the local don turned out to be Ali's enemy, and before he could pull the trigger, he was shot by Ali. Money can't buy loyalty, only deeds can, and this was why Ram was so loyal to his benefactor.

In the event of an emergency, please assume the bracing position. Lean forward with your hands on top of your head and your elbows against your thighs. Ensure your feet are flat on the floor. Should the cabin experience sudden pressure loss, stay calm and listen for instructions from the cabin crew. Oxygen masks will drop down from above your seat. Place the mask over your mouth and nose, like this.

A strange feeling besieged Ram and he felt lost. He realized that he would never return to India. But Ali's last words soothed him and gave him hope. When Ram's mother was seriously ill, Ali had had her admitted to Lilavati Hospital and paid the charges for her radiation. He also helped Ram's sister with her education and got her a seat in a good college. In return, Ram did everything to keep Ali happy. He became Ali's trump card and moved up through his ranks at a rapid pace. Seeing his valour, Ali had chosen him to fulfil his most precious mission and Ram being his faithful follower could not ignore his orders.

Pull the strap to tighten it. If you are travelling with children, make sure that your own mask is on first before helping your children. In the unlikely event of an emergency landing and evacuation, leave your carry-on items behind. A life vest is located in a pouch under your seat or between the armrests. When instructed to do so, open the plastic pouch and remove the vest. Slip it over your head. Pass the straps around your waist and adjust at the front. To inflate the vest, pull firmly on the red cord, only when leaving the aircraft. If you need to refill the vest, blow into the mouthpieces.

Ram Johal looked at the hip of one of the air hostesses standing near him.

***

Epilogue

Chaos and Randomness

We ask that you make sure that all carry-on luggage is stowed away safely during the flight. While we wait for take-off, please take a moment to review the safety data in the seat pocket in front of you. We strongly suggest you read it before take-off. If you have any questions, please don't hesitate to ask one of our crew members. We wish you all an enjoyable flight.

Murali didn't bother to check the safety instructions, because he knew very well that his life was soon going to end. His hapless lungs was struggling to breathe life and was fighting against the erratic behaviour of his brain cells. The disease is cruel but in a different sense as it is painless, non-contagious and it slowly paralyzes each and every part of the body while the heart and mind remain sentient till the end.

The runway was cleared for take-off. Captain Abhishek Patil spoke into the microphone *Flight attendants prepare for take-off please.*

The engine started buzzing; the aircraft began its accelerating run along the runway, and within a few minutes, AI 605 was just a tiny speck in the sky, a blip on the radar. Cruising at an altitude of 20,000 feet, at airspeed of 300 miles per hour, AI 605 was flying above the clouds where the air started to thin and it was also getting smoother. Just then, a voice came cutting through the cabin air trying to get some attention of the passengers on board.

Ladies and gentlemen, the Captain has turned off the Fasten Seat Belt sign, and you may now move around the cabin. However, we always recommend keeping your seat belt fastened while you're seated. You may now turn on your electronic devices such as cell phones, and laptops, but we suggest keeping them on airplane mode.

Vinod unbuckled his seat belt, took a comb from his shirt pocket and neatly combed his curly hair to one side, making it look like waves on the sea. Unlike other scientists, he was stylish, scrupulous in his grooming and clothing and looked pleasing.

In a few moments, the flight attendants will be passing through the cabin to offer you hot or cold drinks, as well as a light snack and you can use the monitor in front of you to browse our in-flight entertainment. Now, sit back, relax, and enjoy the flight. Thank you.

Ram Johal adjusted the brightness of his monitor, tapped the touch screen a few times. He was glad to find one of his favourite movies, *How to steal a million.*

The relief pilot, Jatin Doshi, sat near the controls, watching all the glowing buttons and levers in the cockpit. After six hours of smooth flying, fast rivers of air outside shook the plane causing turbulence strong enough to judder a glass of orange juice kept on the tray table. Captain Patil immediately turned the *seat-belt* sign on and spoke briefly *Cabin crew, please be seated. Ladies and gentleman, we are now crossing a zone of turbulence. Please return to your seats and keep your seat belts fastened. Thank you.*

That mild turbulence sent a chill down Ram Johal's spine and made his heart beat faster. He was shocked and surprised as he had never experienced such a feeling before. How strange that a mild turbulence had made his heart pound fiercely, for it had never pounded so fast, even when he killed people for money, when he robbed them at knifepoint, when he raped young girls and when he smuggled drugs. To overcome his feeling, he closed his eyes and took a deep breath to calm his heart.

Meanwhile, in the cockpit, Jatin's eyes were wide with disbelief. He observed that the plane was banking left. He immediately alerted Captain Patil who looked for warning signals on the flight control systems. After a few minutes, the flight started turning and the flight path indicator changed to show the new flight path.

First Officer Rakesh Mehra: *This is unbelievable! What the fuck is happening? Why is it turning? Let me check all the controls … else let's take control and go manual …*

Captain Patil: *Yes … it's turning!! Go manual … Go manual … take control …*

Jatin Doshi: *It's turning and I am not able to control it … something is wrong with the engines!*

Captain Patil: *I think we are entering a holding pattern. We're in manual, right?*

The turn was continuous. AI 605 started flying in circles, losing altitude after every 180 degrees.

Rakesh Mehra: *Man! This is crazy! I can't believe it! I can't believe it! We are losing altitude! We are going down!*

Suddenly, the plane banked at a 45-degree angle.

Captain Patil: *Hold it, hold the gear. Steady! Steady! Keep her steady! Try to push it way up … try …*

At this angle, it was difficult for Patil to regain control.

Jatin Doshi: *Turn it right … Turn it right … balance … balance … you need to balance … it is going out of control.*

Rakesh Mehra: *I am doing it … I am doing it … I'm trying my best … Hang on!*

Captain Patil: *She is banking … 90 degrees … Get her into a nosedive … Get her into a nosedive … we should not lose altitude … we are going down …*

Rakesh Mehra: *I am trying! I am trying! I am trying my best! Hold on …*

Jatin Doshi: *We are losing altitude … we are losing altitude … oh my God!*

Captain Patil: *The angle … watch the angle … What do you see below? Hills? Mountains? Water?*

Rakesh Mehra: *I am trying to keep … I am trying … I see mountains!*

Captain Patil: *Angle … the angle … watch the angle … that's important … We are going to make it!*

Jatin Doshi: *Turn Left! Turn Left! Turn Left! Keep it steady … try to keep it steady …*

Rakesh Mehra: *Now I am turning it right!*

Captain Patil: *We are losing altitude ... Don't let it hit the ground ... We will survive! We will survive!*

AI 605 started to descend at 900 feet per second. Altitude alert and autopilot disengage warnings sounded in quick succession. Though Captain Patil regained control and levelled the wings, the altitude was too low from them to recover.

Jatin Doshi: *Rakesh, we have to do something ... Do you see the danger?*

Captain Patil: *Give it full power! ... Let's go for it ... full power ... Let's try our best!*

Rakesh Mehra: *I am doing my best ... I am trying ... I think ... we are going down ...*

Jatin Doshi: *Okay ... (sobbing) okay!!*

Captain Patil: *We are going down ... We are going down ... I think we are struck ...*

Rakesh Mehra: *I think we are going to crash ... only God can save us ...*

Jatin Doshi: *Everything is fine ... Everything is fine ... we have to ...*

Captain Patil: *We are going to hit the ground ... There's no way out ... Fuck ... ahh ... here we go ... I believe in God ... We are going to hit the ground ... Fuck ... We are going to hit ...*

AI 605 crashed. The impact was tremendous.

All aboard were killed beyond recognition.

The wreckage was located in a remote forest approximately 30 kilometres west of Hyvinkaa, Finland. Even after two weeks of intense search, the flight data recorders were never found.

After two months of investigation, Finnish and Indian Aviation experts submitted a 200-page report titled: ACCIDENT TO AIR INDIA AI 605 BOEING 777-300 AIRCRAFT ON 1ST JANUARY 2016 AT HYVINKAA, FINLAND, explaining what they thought was the cause. However, the actual cause of Flight AI 605's crash remained unsolved. The report emphasised more on "what" had happened rather than "why" which is usually the tougher question to answer. Engine or mechanical failure was ruled out. The accident was covered by the press, and the public demanded action, but it was impossible to figure out the cause. After a few months, the crash site was turned into a memorial enclosed by a fence. The memorial included a 120-foot (to honour the 120 passengers and crew) chain-link fence on which visitors could leave flowers, bouquets, flags and other items. The memorial also included a row of small wooden plaques, one for each passenger or crew member. There were handwritten messages on the railings at the memorial that read, *Why him? He was a noble soul; God! Why did you do this?* along with other messages and quotes etched with grief and despair.

We blame God for everything that happens in this world. We believe that everything happens for a reason. Every event is pre-written in the book of God and we are naught but puppets in his hands. But the fact is, we don't have access to the "Book of God." We can't turn the pages to unveil the future. And we don't have definitive answers to these questions – is God in control of all and everything? Are we dancing and singing to his tune? Is God really pulling the strings? Are we puppets in the hands of destiny? Is everything in this world determined in advance? Is karma real?

If the answer is YES to any of the above questions, then we have to re-evaluate our answers. If God's total sovereignty over all forms of life is true, then why did he crash a plane and kill a scientist who was willing to change the world with his inventions? Why did an honest police officer die? Why were two researchers who had the ability to save lives killed?

Human mind is always obsessed with patterns but randomness comes as a lurking devil, shattering all synonyms of pattern with a mighty blow that stuns those who believe in a deterministic world.

Chaos and randomness are close kin. Where chaos begins, logic stops. Where chaos begins, discipline stops. Where chaos begins, everything stops. Chaos and randomness seem to be present everywhere. We humans are caught up and swept along by the waves of chaos, leaving us bewildered and forcing us to swim out of the strong current of anarchy to find a way through riotous confusion and disorder.

Chaos is the pulse of the universe. It can be seen in the bizarre formation of clouds. It is evident in the weather. It grinned when AI 605 banked to its left for no reason and ended up crashing.

Is there a way to deal with Randomness and Chaos?

Can Probability and Statistics save us from this chaotic world?

Can mathematical models be used to predict the future?

Though we don't have a definite answer to these questions, we have been trying to find a pattern to beat randomness. We want to connect the dots and seek patterns. Our human mind has a tendency to find meaning in otherwise meaningless data.

Keeping aside the technical reasons behind the crash of Air India Flight 605, let's hear it from those who believe in a pre-written, deterministic world where everything happens for a reason and all events and rules are governed by God. Theologians would say God crashed the flight on purpose as Ram Johal – the notorious criminal was on board and was travelling to New York to explode a bomb that could kill innocent civilians.

Will God crash a flight to kill one criminal along with 119 innocent lives?

The absence of logic or pattern or purpose behind the plane crash is clearly evident when we scan the profile of some of the passengers who boarded Air India Flight 605. A look at Sudhir's adventurous past and the key events that took place in his life alters all that we know about what should happen and what shouldn't. Sudhir played with death all his life and had been in dangerous situations all through his twenty years of playing with high altitudes and venomous snakes. But when he was embracing life, death came in like a thief through a plane crash and took his life away at uncommon hours.

A scientist, who had the potential to make the world a better place, was killed.

An experienced police officer, so full of life, who was carrying his dreams on his shoulders, was suddenly diagnosed with a progressive neurodegenerative disease. He was travelling overseas to find a cure for ALS, but fate won against faith, bringing his life to an abrupt end.

In a world full of uncertainties, randomness and chaos seem to be the norm. Mathematicians dealing with probability and statistics are finding it hard to tame chaotic randomness. For what is going to happen in the future is always thought and conceived by an inquisitive mind which either brings in the concept of God who is behind all and everything that happens in this universe or science that is tirelessly trying to unravel the mysteries of tomorrow with the knowledge of yesterday and today. Astronomers say that our own sun will turn into a red giant star and will eventually engulf earth before collapsing into a white dwarf. Cosmologists predict that the ever-expanding universe will one day shrink into a dimensionless singularity, turning everything real into a cosmic dream. For all events that happen in this universe are naught but a play directed by randomness and chaos, and we mortals can either look at it with awe or lament before the grave of the dead.

*** The End ***

References & Bibliography

This book is a work of fiction. In some places, facts are interspersed with fiction to make the plot realistic. All the reference materials cited below were used to give intensity to the story.

References

- Website of Department of Science and Technology (http://www.dst.gov.in) was referred to know about India's stance on science and technology.

- Website of American Psychological Association (http://www.apa.org) was referred as the plot deals with aspects related to psychological disorders like depression.

- Apart from referring Wikipedia to know facts related to Depression, the following link was used to learn more about the disease. https://www.dosomething. org/us/facts/11-facts-about-depression. Content of this link has collective information gathered from World Health Organization (WHO) and American Psychological Association (APA) on Depression and other mental disorders.

- The quote on page 35 - *In a time not distant, it will be possible to flash any image formed in thought on a screen and render it visible at any place desired* – was told by Nikola Tesla, Serbian–American Inventor.

- https://en.wikipedia.org/wiki/Arthur_Road_Jail was used to gather facts related to Arthur Road Jail.

- https://mumbaipolice.maharashtra.gov.in/crimebranch.asp – Website of Mumbai Police – was referred to know about Anti-Narcotics Branch.

- https://en.wikipedia.org/wiki/Thought_identification – was referred to know about the concept of thought identification.

- The quote *THOUGHT IS YOUR ENEMY* on page 84 was told by Philosopher U.G. Krishnamurti.

- http://theweek.com/articles/444418/how-snake-venom-could-help-fight-cancer – Article written by Eli Chen on August 25th 2014 was referred to know about therapeutic effects of snake venom. Also, Wikipedia page about King Cobra was referred to learn about king cobras.

- Haditoxin was discovered in Professor Manjunatha Kini's laboratory at the National University of Singapore. Co-author of the paper, Dr S. Niru Nirthanan, now at Griffith University on the Gold Coast, has characterised the pharmacological actions of haditoxin. http://esciencenews.com/articles/2010/03/08/snake.venom.charms.science.world – This link was referred to learn about haditoxin.

- Website of ALS Association (http://www.alsa.org) was referred to know about ALS disease.

- https://en.wikipedia.org/wiki/List_of_Islamist_terrorist_attacks – This link was referred to know about Islamic terror attacks.

- https://en.wikipedia.org/wiki/Dirty_bomb – This link was referred to know about dirty bombs.

Bibliography

- Cabin Safety Inspectors Handbook, Government of India, Civil Aviation Department, Cabin Safety Division, DGCA, India – August 2013 – Rev 4.

- "How Quantum Computers Work" by Kevin Bonsor & Jonathan Strickland, dated: 4/2/16, covered in howstuffworks.com.

- Mechelli, A., Price, C.J., Friston, K.J. & Ashburner, J. (2005). "Voxel-Based Morphometry of the Human Brain: Methods and Applications." *Current Medical Imaging Review.*

- *Dice World* by Brian Clegg – Published in UK in 2013 by Icon Books Ltd.

My Previous Books

The Peak of all Thoughts
Vijay Raghav

About the Book: "You say, my words for now have dressed themselves as pixels and print-inks and can warm a heart! Verily, I have written them with my own blood with a glowing fire in my heart!"

The Peak of all Thoughts is a book of 32 poetic essays which capture the conversations between the man behind the peak thought and the drones that are earthly beings. The man behind the peak thought answers the queries thrown at him by earthly beings and their conversation covers various aspects of life written in prose–poetry style.

Synopsis: *The Peak of all Thoughts* is a book of 32 poetic essays which captures the exchange of words, ideas and philosophy between the poetic persona and men of doubts, confusions of the muddy mundane world. The man behind the peak unveils the queries thrown at him.

Much like *The Prophet* of Khalil Gibran, the short and pithy tales unfold the root cause of human pathos, solve the mystery with artistic mastery and finally reach a universal solution, which is certainly sublime to attain.

The author's prophetic take over the topics he deals with often reminds the readers of the Biblical parables, not in the pious moralistic tone, but in the simplicity of language, ease of communication and lucidity of expression. Poetry is the medium of language, which simply communicates the most profound truth in the core of human heart. The parables also are so poetic in their theme, tone and texture, that they convey their essence as clear as water and as deep as the same.

Fall
Publisher: Leadstart Publishers
Vijay Raghav

About the Book: This is a novel for people whose consciousness involves feeling and sensibility. It explores the impact of "Emotions" in one's life. It has the pace of a thriller and the mysteriousness of a sweet romance. It is a novel etched with a bouquet of poetic essays. There is poetry and puzzle. The characters are wickedly intelligent but sometimes they act according to the impulse of the moment. *Fall* is a heady mixture of love, envy, murder, deceit and mystery. Are you ready to experience too many good things at once? If yes, then read through the pages intoxicated with love. Once you finish the book, you'll be drunk with emotions and will be weary to speak in words!

Synopsis of the Book: Jules Verne, Assistant Professor of Mathematics at Lyon College, wakes up to a regular day of teaching sessions at college. However, the day turns out to be like no other he has ever experienced when he finds a dead man lying in a pool of his own blood with his throat slit open. Who is the dead man? Who has killed him? What is the motive behind the murder?

Frederick, a budding poet, achieves success on the literary front with his book *Autumn Leaves* receiving public adulation. He meets his love, Claire; they plan to get married. Will destiny unite them in matrimonial bliss?

Another murder is committed in Grenoble. Inspector Marc is appointed to investigate the murder. What he discovers is an intricately woven plot to deceive and kill.

Set in France, *Fall* is a riveting story of love, envy, deceit and mystery – a fascinating read.